CHILDREN'S STORIES FROM DICKENS

CHILDREN'S STORIES
FROM DICKENS

Retold by his Granddaughter
Mary Angela Dickens

Illustrated by Harold Copping

Derrydale Books
New York • Avenel, New Jersey

This edition
Copyright © 1993 by Outlet Book Company, Inc.

All rights reserved. First published in 1993 by Derrydale Books, dis-
tributed by Outlet Book Company, Inc., a Random House Company, 40 Engelhard Avenue, Avenel, New Jersey 07001

Random House
New York • Toronto • London • Sydney • Auckland
Designed by Eileen Rosenthal
Printed and bound in the Singapore

Library of Congress Cataloging-in-Publication Data
Dickens, Mary Angela. Children's stories from Dickens / by Mary
Angela Dickens ; illustrated by Harold Copping. p.   cm. Summary:
Retells the stories of Charles Dickens's most famous child characters,
including Oliver Twist, David Copperfield, and Little Nell.
    ISBN 0-517-08485-6 : $8.99   1. Children's stories, English.
[1. England—Fiction.   2. Short stories.]   I. Dickens, Charles, 1812–
    1870.   II. Copping, Harold, ill.   III. Title.
    PZ7.D5525Ch 1993 [Fic]—dc20 92-37666 CIP AC

8   7   6   5   4   3   2   1

Contents
❀

Introduction 7

Oliver Twist 9

Jenny Wren 34

Tiny Tim 40

Little David Copperfield 47

The Blind Toymaker 65

Little Paul Dombey 72

The Marchioness 82

The Fat Boy 92

Little Dorrit of the Marshalsea 100

Little Nell and her Grandfather 110

Introduction

CHARLES DICKENS, who was born in 1812, is considered one of the greatest of English novelists. Certainly he is the most popular. Not only did he have an important place in nineteenth-century literature, but he was also an outspoken and influential critic of society. He wrote fifteen novels as well as a number of stories and Christmas books. In lots of these children were important characters.

In his day, no one understood children better than Dickens, and he was the first writer to describe what children thought and felt and to capture the way they spoke. And he was not afraid to write about the hard and sad lives that many children led.

In the stories in this book, which have been retold by Charles Dickens's granddaughter, Mary Angela Dickens, you will meet some of the children who appear in the works of Charles Dickens.

There is Oliver Twist, who had many misadventures after he escaped from the terrible workhouse where he was born, and David Copperfield, the hero of Dickens's most popular novel, much of which records his own experiences. Little Paul Dombey is the young son of *Dombey and Son,* and Amy is the heroine of *Little Dorrit.*

On these pages you'll also make the acquaintance of Tiny Tim, from *A Christmas Carol,* the fat boy from *The Pickwick Papers,* Jenny Wren from *Our Mutual Friend,* the blind little toymaker from *The Cricket on the Hearth,* and Little Nell and the Marchioness from *The Old Curiosity Shop.*

Howard Copping's wonderful paintings and drawings bring Dickens's fascinating characters, both young and old, to life.

Oliver Twist

Once upon a time there was born in a country workhouse a baby boy. He was a poor, weakly little child, and at the time of his birth his mother died, and nobody knew who she was, and nobody had heard of his father or any of his relations, so he was just a poor little atom in this wide, wide world of ours.

The workhouse people called him Oliver Twist, and brought him up with a lot of other miserable children who were also without fathers or mothers. The poor boy was beaten and half-starved, and was altogether as unhappy as unhappy can be.

The room in which the boys were fed was a large stone hall, with a copper at one end, out of which the master, dressed in an apron for the purpose, and assisted by one or two women, ladled the gruel at meal times. Of this festive composition each boy had one porringer, and no more—except on occasions of great public rejoicing, when he had two ounces and a quarter of bread besides. The bowls never needed washing. The boys polished them with their spoons till they shone again. And, when they had performed this operation (which never took very long, the spoons being nearly as large as the bowls), they would sit staring at the copper with such eager eyes as if they could have devoured the very bricks of which it was composed, employing themselves meanwhile in sucking their fingers most assiduously, with the view of catching up any stray splashes of gruel that might have been cast thereon.

Boys have generally excellent appetites. Oliver Twist and his companions suffered the tortures of slow starvation for several months; at last they got so voracious and wild with hunger that one boy, who was tall for his age, and hadn't been used to that sort of thing (for his father had kept a small cook-shop), hinted darkly to his companions that unless he had another basin of gruel each day he was afraid he might some night happen to eat the boy who slept next him, who happened to be a weakly youth of tender age. He had a wild, hungry eye, and they implicitly believed him. A council was held. Lots were cast who should walk up to the master after supper that evening, and ask for more. It fell to Oliver.

The evening arrived. The boys took their places. The master, in his cook's uniform, stationed himself at the copper, his pauper assistants ranged themselves behind him, the gruel was served out, and a long grace

was said over the short commons. The gruel disappeared. The boys whispered to each other and winked at Oliver, while his next neighbors nudged him. Child as he was, he was desperate with hunger and reckless with misery. He rose from the table, and, advancing to the master, basin and spoon in hand, said, somewhat alarmed at his own temerity, "Please, sir, I want some more."

The master was a fat, healthy man, but he turned very pale. He gazed in stupefied astonishment at the small rebel for some seconds, and then clung for support to the copper. The assistants were paralyzed with wonder, the boys with fear.

"What!" said the master at length, in a faint voice.

"Please, sir," replied Oliver, "I want some more."

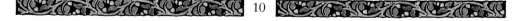

The master aimed a blow at Oliver's head with the ladle, pinioned him in his arms, and shrieked aloud for the beadle.

The board was sitting in solemn conclave, when Mr. Bumble, the beadle, rushed into the room in great excitement, and addressing the gentleman in the high chair, said, "Mr. Limbkins, I beg your pardon, sir! Oliver Twist has asked for more!"

There was a general start. Horror was depicted on every countenance.

"For *more!*" said Mr. Limbkins. "Compose yourself, Bumble, and answer me distinctly. Do I understand that he asked for more after he had eaten the supper allotted by the dietary?"

"He did, sir," replied Bumble.

"That boy will be hung," said a gentleman in a white waistcoat. "I know that boy will be hung."

Nobody controverted the prophetic gentleman's opinion. An animated discussion took place. Oliver was ordered into instant confinement, and a bill was next morning pasted on the outside of the gate offering a reward of five pounds to anybody who would take Oliver Twist off the hands of the parish. In other words, five pounds and Oliver Twist were offered to any man or woman who wanted an apprentice to any trade, business or calling.

Well, the bill on the gate had its effect, and Oliver, at the early age of ten, left the workhouse to earn his living. He was apprenticed to an undertaker called Mr. Sowerberry, and here he was as badly treated as he had been at the workhouse. Mr. Sowerberry had another apprentice, named Noah Claypole, who was a horrid, disagreeable boy. He and the servant Charlotte were continually bullying poor little Oliver.

One day Noah went too far. He abused Oliver's mother.

"Work'us," said Noah—he always called Oliver "Work'us"—"how's your mother?"

"She's dead," replied Oliver. "Don't you say anything about her to me!"

Oliver's color rose as he said this, he breathed quickly, and there was a curious working of the mouth and nostrils, which Mr. Claypole thought must be the immediate precursor of a violent fit of crying. Under this impression he returned to the charge.

"What did she die of, Work'us?" said Noah.

"Of a broken heart some of our old nurses told me," replied Oliver, more as if he were talking to himself than answering Noah. "I think I know what it must be to die of that!"

"Tol de rol lol lol, right fol lairy, Work'us," said Noah, as a tear rolled down Oliver's cheek. "What's set you a-sniveling now?"

"Not *you*," replied Oliver, hastily brushing the tear away. "Don't think it."

"Oh, not me, eh?" sneered Noah.

"No, not you," replied Oliver sharply. "There, that's enough. Don't say anything more to me about her; you'd better not!"

"Better not!" exclaimed Noah. "Well! Better not! Work'us, don't be impudent. *Your* mother, too! She was a nice 'un, she was. Oh, Lor!" And here Noah nodded his head expressively, and curled up as much of his small red nose as muscular action could collect together for the occasion.

"Yer know, Work'us," continued Noah, emboldened by Oliver's silence, and speaking in a jeering tone of affected pity—of all tones the most annoying—"yer know, Work'us, it can't be helped now, and of course yer couldn't help it then, and I'm very sorry for it, and I'm sure we all are, and pity yer very much. But yer must know, Work'us, yer mother was a regular right-down bad 'un."

"What did you say?" inquired Oliver, looking up very quickly.

"A right-down bad 'un, Work'us," replied Noah, coolly. "And it's a great deal better, Work'us, that she died when she did, or else, she'd have been hard laboring in Bridewell, or transported, or hung, which is more likely than either, isn't it?"

Crimson with fury, Oliver started up, overthrew the chair and table, seized Noah by the throat, shook him in the violence of his rage till his

teeth chattered in his head, and, collecting his whole force into one heavy blow, felled him to the ground.

A minute ago the boy had looked the quiet, mild, dejected creature that harsh treatment had made him. But his spirit was roused at last. The cruel insult to his dead mother had set his blood on fire. His breast heaved. His attitude was erect. His eye bright and vivid. His whole person changed, as he stood glaring over the cowardly tormentor who now lay crouching at his feet, and defied him with an energy he had never known before.

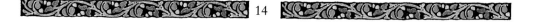

"He'll murder me!" blubbered Noah. "Charlotte! Missis! Here's the new boy a-murdering of me! Help! help! Oliver's gone mad! Charlotte!"

Noah's shouts were responded to by a loud scream from Charlotte and a louder scream from Mrs. Sowerberry, the former of whom rushed into the kitchen by a side door, while the latter paused on the staircase till she was quite certain that it was consistent with the preservation of human life to come further down.

"Oh, you little wretch!" screamed Charlotte, seizing Oliver with her utmost force, which was about equal to that of a moderately strong man in particularly good training. "Oh, you little un-grate-ful, mur-de-rous, hor-rid villain!" And between every syllable Charlotte gave Oliver a blow with all her might, accompanying it with a scream.

Charlotte's fist was by no means a light one; but, lest it should not be effectual in calming Oliver's wrath, Mrs. Sowerberry plunged into the kitchen and assisted to hold him with one hand while she scratched his face with the other. In this favorable position of affairs Noah rose from the ground and pummeled him behind.

This was rather too violent exercise to last long. When they were all three wearied out and could tear and beat no longer, they dragged Oliver, struggling and shouting, but not daunted, into the dust cellar, and there locked him up. This being done, Mrs. Sowerberry sank into a chair and burst into tears.

"Bless her, she's going off!" said Charlotte. "A glass of water, Noah, dear. Make haste!"

"Oh! Charlotte," said Mrs. Sowerberry, speaking as well as she could through a deficiency of breath and a sufficiency of cold water, which Noah had poured over her head and shoulders. "Oh! Charlotte, what a mercy we have not all been murdered in our beds!"

"Ah! Mercy indeed, ma'am," was the reply. "I only hope this'll teach master not to have any more of these dreadful creatures that are born to be murderers and robbers from their very cradle. Poor Noah! He was all but killed, ma'am, when I come in."

"Poor fellow!" said Mrs. Sowerberry, looking pityingly on the charity boy.

Noah, whose top waistcoat button might have been somewhere on a level with the crown of Oliver's head, rubbed his eyes with the inside of his wrists while this commiseration was bestowed upon him, and performed some affecting tears and sniffs.

"What's to be done?" exclaimed Mrs. Sowerberry. "Your master's not at home, there's not a man in the house, and he'll kick that door down in ten minutes." Oliver's vigorous plunges against the bit of timber in question rendered this occurrence highly probable.

"Dear, dear! I don't know, ma'am," said Charlotte, "unless we send for the police officers."

"Or the millingtary," suggested Mr. Claypole.

"No, no," said Mrs. Sowerberry, bethinking herself of the beadle. "Run to Mr. Bumble, Noah, and tell him to come here directly, and not to lose a minute. Never mind your cap! Make haste! You can hold a knife to that black eye as you run along. It'll keep the swelling down."

Noah did not stop to reply, but started off at his fullest speed; and very much it astonished the people who were out walking to see a charity boy tearing through the streets pell-mell, with no cap on his head and a clasp-knife at his eye.

Poor Oliver was terribly punished for this, so much so that he determined to run away. But it was not until he was left alone in the silence and stillness of the gloomy workshop of the undertaker that Oliver gave way to the feelings which the day's treatment may be supposed likely to have awakened in a mere child. He had listened to their taunts with a look of contempt. He had borne the lash without a cry, for he felt that pride swelling in his heart which would have kept down a shriek to the last, though they had roasted him alive. But now, when there was none to see or hear him, he fell upon his knees on the floor, and, hiding his face in his hands, wept such tears as, God send for the credit of our nature, few so young may ever have cause to pour out before Him!

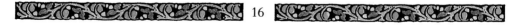

For a long time Oliver remained motionless in this attitude. The candle was burning low in the socket when he rose to his feet. Having gazed cautiously round him and listened intently, he gently undid the fastenings of the door and looked abroad.

It was a cold, dark night. The stars seemed to the boy's eyes farther from the earth than he had ever seen them before. There was no wind, and the somber shadows thrown by the trees upon the ground looked sepulchral and deathlike from being so still. He softly reclosed the door. Having availed himself of the expiring light of the candle to tie up in a handkerchief the few articles of wearing apparel he had, he sat himself down upon a bench to wait for morning.

With the first ray of light that struggled through the crevices in the shutters Oliver arose, and again unbarred the door. One timid look around, one moment's pause of hesitation; he had closed it behind him, and was in the open street.

He looked to the right and to the left, uncertain whither to fly. He remembered to have seen the wagons as they went out toiling up the hill. He took the same route, and, arriving at a footpath across the fields, which he knew after some distance led out again into the road, struck into it, and walked quickly on.

Along this same footpath Oliver well remembered he had trotted beside Mr. Bumble, the beadle. His heart beat quickly when he remembered this, and he half resolved to turn back. He had come a long way, though, and should lose a great deal of time by doing so. Besides, it was so early that there was very little fear of his being seen, so he walked on.

He reached a house. There was no appearance of its inmates stirring at that early hour. Oliver stopped and peeped into the garden. A child was weeding one of the little beds. As he stopped, he raised his pale face and disclosed the features of one of his former companions. Oliver felt glad to see him before he went, for, though younger than himself, he had been his little friend and playmate. They had been beaten and starved and shut up together many and many a time.

OLIVER TWIST

"Hush, Dick!" said Oliver, as the boy ran to the gate and thrust his thin arm between the rails to greet him. "Is anyone up?"

"Nobody but me," replied the child.

"You mustn't say you saw me, Dick," said Oliver. "I am running away. They beat and ill-use me, Dick, and I am going to seek my fortune some long way off. I don't know where. How pale you are!"

"I heard the doctor tell them I was dying," replied the child with a faint smile. "I am very glad to see you; but don't stop, don't stop!"

"Yes, yes, I will, to say good-bye to you," replied Oliver. "I shall see you again, Dick. I know I shall! You will be well and happy!"

"I hope so," replied the child. "After I am dead, but not before. I know the doctor must be right, Oliver, because I dream so much of heaven and angels and kind faces that I never see when I am awake. Kiss me," said the child, climbing up the low gate and flinging his little arms round Oliver's neck. "Good-bye! God bless you!"

The blessing was from a young child's lips, but it was the first that Oliver had ever heard invoked upon his head, and through the struggles and sufferings and troubles and changes of his later life he never once forgot it.

So this poor, friendless boy trudged off to London. He had no idea what he was going to do, where he was going to sleep, or when he would have his next meal. All he wanted was to get away from the cruel, unhappy life he had been leading.

Unfortunately, Oliver was to suffer worse miseries. For seven weary days he begged his way, sleeping under haystacks and other such places, and was nearly dying of starvation and hunger when he met a strange boy. This boy, who was some years older than Oliver, gave him something to eat, and then took him to his home.

It was an awful home this, where the boy took Oliver, and awful people lived in it—horrible, wicked people, who lived entirely by stealing. Oliver was an innocent lad, and did not discover for some time that he was living with thieves. But one day he was out with the boy who had

18

taken him home and another boy, when they saw an old gentleman standing by a bookstall. Immediately the two boys who were with Oliver walked stealthily across the road and slunk close behind the old gentleman. Oliver walked a few paces after them, and not knowing whether to advance or retire, stood looking on in silent amazement.

The old gentleman was a very respectable-looking personage, with a powdered head and gold spectacles. He was dressed in a bottle-green coat with a black velvet collar, wore white trousers, and carried a smart bamboo cane under his arm. He had taken a book from the stall; and there he stood reading away as hard as if he were in his armchair in his own study. It is very possible that he fancied himself there indeed, for it was plain, from his utter abstraction, that he saw not the bookstall, nor the street, nor the boys, nor, in short, anything but the book itself, which he was reading straight through, turning over the leaf when he got to the bottom of a page, beginning at the top line of the next one and going regularly on with the greatest interest and eagerness.

What was Oliver's horror and alarm, as he stood a few paces off, looking on with his eyelids as wide open as they would possibly go, to see one of the boys plunge his hand into the old gentleman's pocket, and draw from there a handkerchief! To see him hand the same to the other boy, and finally to behold them both running away round the corner at full speed!

Oliver stood for a moment with the blood so tingling through all his veins from terror that he felt as if he were in a burning fire, then, confused and frightened, he took to his heels, and not knowing what he did, made off as fast as he could lay his feet to the ground.

This was all done in a minute's space. In the very instant when Oliver began to run, the old gentleman, putting his hand to his pocket and missing his handkerchief, turned sharp round. Seeing the boy scudding away at such a rapid pace he very naturally concluded him to be the culprit, and, shouting "Stop thief!" with all his might, made off after him, book in hand.

But the old gentleman was not the only person who raised the hue and cry. The two young thieves, unwilling to attract public attention by running down the open street, had merely retired into the very first doorway round the corner. They no sooner heard the cry and saw Oliver running than, guessing exactly how the matter stood, they issued forth with great promptitude, and, shouting "Stop thief!" too, joined in the pursuit like good citizens.

Although Oliver had been brought up by philosophers he was not theoretically acquainted with the beautiful axiom that self-preservation is the first law of nature. If he had been, perhaps he would have been prepared for this. Not being prepared, however, it alarmed him the more; so away he went like the wind, with the old gentleman and the two boys roaring and shouting behind him.

"Stop thief! Stop thief!" There is a magic in the sound. The tradesman leaves his counter and the carman his wagon, the butcher throws down his tray, the baker his basket, the milkman his pail, the errand boy his parcels, the schoolboy his marbles, the paver his pickaxe, the child his battledore. Away they run, pell-mell helter-skelter, slap-dash, tearing, yelling and screaming, knocking down the passengers as they turn the corners, rousing up the dogs and astonishing the fowls; and streets, squares and courts re-echo with the sound.

"Stop thief! Stop thief!" The cry is taken up by a hundred voices, and the crowd accumulates at every turning. Away they fly, splashing through the mud and rattling along the pavements; up go the windows, out run the people, onward tears the mob, a whole audience desert Punch in the very thickest of the plot, and joining the rushing throng swell the shout, and lend fresh vigor to the cry—

"Stop thief! Stop thief!"

"Stop thief! Stop thief!" There is a passion for hunting something deeply implanted in the human breast. One wretched, breathless child, panting with exhaustion, terror in his looks, agony in his eyes, large drops of perspiration streaming down his face, strains every nerve to make head upon his pursuers, and as they follow on his track and gain upon him every instant they hail his decreasing strength with still louder shouts, and whoop and scream with joy, "Stop thief!"

Stopped at last! A clever blow! He is down upon the pavement, and

the crowd eagerly gather round him, each newcomer jostling and struggling with the others to catch a glimpse.

"Stand aside!"

"Give him a little air!"

"Nonsense, he don't deserve it!"

"Where's the gentleman?"

"Here he is, coming down the street."

"Make room there for the gentleman!"

"Is this the boy, sir?"

"Yes."

Oliver lay, covered with mud and dust, and bleeding from the mouth, looking wildly round upon the heap of faces that surrounded him, when the old gentleman was officiously dragged and pushed into the circle by the foremost of the pursuers.

"Yes," said the gentleman, "I am afraid it is the boy."

"Afraid!" murmured the crowd. "That's a good 'un."

"Poor fellow!" said the gentleman, "he has hurt himself."

"*I* did that, sir," said a great lubberly fellow, stepping forward, "and preciously *I* cut my knuckle agin' his mouth. *I* stopped him, sir."

The fellow touched his hat with a grin, expecting something for his pains, but the old gentleman, eyeing him with an expression of dislike, looked anxiously round as if he contemplated running away himself, which it is very possible he might have attempted to do, and thus afforded another chase, had not a police officer (who is generally the last person to arrive in such cases) at that moment made his way through the crowd, and seized Oliver by the collar.

"Come, get up!" said the man roughly.

"It wasn't me, indeed, sir! Indeed, indeed, it was two other boys," said Oliver, clasping his hands passionately, and looking round. "They are here somewhere."

"Oh, no, they ain't," said the officer. He meant this to be ironical, but it was true besides, for the real thieves had filed off down the first

convenient court they came to. "Come, get up!" he repeated.

"Don't hurt him," said the old gentleman compassionately.

"Oh, no, I won't hurt him," replied the officer, tearing his jacket half off his back in proof thereof. "Come, I know you. It won't do. Will you stand upon your legs?"

Oliver, who could hardly stand, made a shift to raise himself on his feet, and was at once lugged along the streets by the jacket collar at a rapid pace. The gentleman walked on with them by the officer's side, and as many of the crowd as could achieve the feat got a little ahead and stared back at Oliver from time to time. The boys shouted in triumph, and on they went.

Poor Oliver was taken before a magistrate, and was tried and sentenced to go to prison for three months. The police were taking the boy away when an elderly man of decent but poor appearance, clad in an old suit of black, rushed hastily into the office, and advanced toward the magistrate.

"Stop! stop! Don't take him away! For heaven's sake, stop a moment!" cried the newcomer, breathless with haste.

"I saw three boys," continued the man, "two others and the prisoner here, loitering on the opposite side of the way when this gentleman was reading. The robbery was committed by another boy. I saw it done, and I saw that this boy was perfectly amazed and stupefied by it." Having by this time recovered a little breath, the worthy bookstall-keeper proceeded to relate, in a more coherent manner, the exact circumstances of the robbery.

So it happened that Oliver did not go to prison, but instead was taken home by the old gentleman who had been robbed, and was tenderly cared for. Indeed, Oliver was happy for the first time in his life.

It would be very nice to be able to tell you that Oliver stayed with this kind old gentleman; but, alas! It was not so. Those wicked thieves stole Oliver away, and took him back to their awful home, and threatened to kill him if he ran away again.

Among these thieves there was one more desperate and wicked than the others. His name was Bill Sikes. Well, one night Sikes and another man went out to rob a house, and took Oliver with them to help, poor boy!

When they came to the house, which was in the country, Sikes, who was in the garden, put Oliver gently through a little window, and told him to go and open the street door and let them in.

"Take this lantern," said Sikes. "You see the stairs afore you?"

Oliver, more dead than alive, gasped out, "Yes." Sikes, pointing to the street door with the pistol barrel, briefly advised him to take notice that he was well within shot all the way, and that if he faltered he would fall dead that instant.

"It's done in a minute," said Sikes, in the same low whisper. "Directly I leave go of you you do your work. Hark!"

"What's that?" whispered the other man.

They listened intently.

"Nothing," said Sikes, releasing his hold of Oliver. "Now!"

In the short time he had had to collect his senses the boy had firmly resolved that, whether he died in the attempt or not, he would make one effort to dart upstairs from the hall and alarm the family.

Filled with this idea he advanced at once, but stealthily.

"Come back!" suddenly cried Sikes aloud. "Back! back!"

Scared by the sudden breaking of the dead stillness of the place, and by a loud cry which followed it, Oliver let his lantern fall, and knew not whether to advance or fly.

The cry was repeated. A light appeared. A vision of two terrified half-dressed men at the top of the stairs swam before his eyes. There was a flash—a loud noise—a smoke—a crash somewhere, but where he knew not—and he staggered back.

Sikes muttered horribly to himself, grinding his teeth with rage, as he hurried along. Then for a moment he rested the body of the wounded

boy across his bended knee, and turned his head for an instant to look back at his pursuers.

There was little to be made out in the mist and darkness; but the loud shouting of men vibrated through the air, and the barking of the neighboring dogs, roused by the sound of the alarm bell, resounded in every direction.

"Stop, you hound!" cried the robber, shouting after the other burglar, Toby Crackit, who, making the best use of his long legs, was already ahead—"Stop!"

The repetition of the word brought Toby to a dead standstill, for he was not quite satisfied that he was beyond the range of pistol shot, and Sikes was in no mood to be played with.

"Bear a hand with the boy," roared Sikes, beckoning furiously to his confederate. "Come back!"

Toby made a show of returning, but ventured in a low voice, broken for want of breath to intimate considerable reluctance as he came slowly along.

"Quicker!" cried Sikes, laying the boy in a dry ditch at his feet, and drawing a pistol from his pocket. "Don't play the booby with me."

At this moment the noise grew louder, and Sikes again looking round could discern that the men who had given chase were already climbing the gate of the field in which he stood, and that a couple of dogs were some paces in advance of them.

"It's all up, Bill," cried Toby. "Drop the kid and show 'em your heels."

With this parting advice, Mr. Crackit, preferring the chance of being shot by his friend to the certainty of being taken by his enemies, fairly turned tail, and darted off at full speed.

Sikes clenched his teeth, took one look round, threw over the prostrate form of Oliver the cape in which he had been hurriedly muffled, ran along the front of the hedge as if to distract the attention of those behind from the spot where the boy lay, paused for a second before another

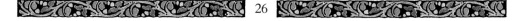

hedge which met it at right angles, and whirling his pistol high into the air, cleared it at a bound, and was gone.

"Ho, ho, there!" cried a tremulous voice in the rear. "Pincher, Neptune, come here, come here!"

The dogs, which in common with their masters seemed to have no particular relish for the sport in which they were engaged, readily answered to this command, and three men, who had by this time advanced some distance into the field, stopped to take counsel together.

The result of their talk was that they returned to their home without finding poor Oliver. As a matter of fact, they were all very nervous, for it's by no means a pleasant thing to have to turn out of a warm bed on a cold night to hunt armed burglars—desperate, wicked men who would not hesitate to shoot you.

◆ ◆ ◆

The air grew colder as day came slowly on, and the mist rolled along the ground like a dense cloud of smoke. The grass was wet, the pathways and low places were all mire and water, and the damp breath of an unwholesome wind went languidly by with a hollow moaning. Still Oliver lay motionless and insensible on the spot where Sikes had left him.

Morning drew on apace. The air became more sharp and piercing as its first dull hue—the death of night rather than the birth of day—glimmered faintly in the sky. The objects which had looked dim and terrible in the darkness grew more and more defined, and gradually resolved into their familiar shapes. The rain came down thick and fast, and pattered noisily among the leafless bushes. But Oliver felt it not as it beat against him, for he still lay stretched, helpless and unconscious, on his bed of clay.

At length a low cry of pain broke the stillness that prevailed, and, uttering it, the boy awoke. His left arm, rudely bandaged in a shawl, hung heavy and useless at his side, and the bandage was saturated with blood.

 28

He was so weak that he could scarcely raise himself into a sitting posture and when he had done so, he looked feebly round for help, and groaned with pain. Trembling in every joint from cold and exhaustion, he made an effort to stand upright, but shuddering from head to foot, fell prostrate on the ground.

After a short return of the stupor in which he had been so long plunged, Oliver, urged by a creeping sickness at his heart, which seemed to warn him that if he lay there he must surely die, got upon his feet and tried to walk.

His head was dizzy, and he staggered to and fro like a drunken man, but he kept up nevertheless, and, with his head drooping languidly on his breast, went stumbling onward he knew not where.

And now hosts of bewildering and confusing ideas came crowding on his mind. He seemed to be still walking between Sikes and Crackit, who were angrily disputing, for the very words they said sounded in his ears. And when he caught his own attention, as it were, by making some violent effort to save himself from falling, he found that he was talking to them.

Then he was alone with Sikes, plodding on as they had done the previous day, and as shadowy people passed them by, he felt the robber's grasp upon his wrist. Suddenly he started back at the report of firearms, and there rose into the air loud cries and shouts; lights gleamed before his eyes, and all was noise and tumult as some unseen hand bore him hurriedly away. Through all these rapid visions there ran an undefined, uneasy consciousness of pain, which wearied and tormented him incessantly.

Thus he staggered on, creeping almost mechanically between the bars of gates or through hedge gaps as they came in his way, until he reached a road. And here the rain began to fall so heavily that it roused him.

He looked about, and saw that at no great distance there was a house, which perhaps he could reach. Seeing his condition they might have

compassion on him, and if they did not it would be better, he thought, to die near human beings than in the lonely open fields.

He summoned up all his strength for one last trial, and bent his faltering steps towards it.

As he drew nearer to this house a feeling came over him that he had seen it before. He remembered nothing of its details, but the shape and aspect of the building seemed familiar to him.

That garden wall! On the grass inside he had fallen on his knees last night and prayed the two men's mercy. It was the very same house they had attempted to rob. Oliver felt such fear come over him when he recognized the place, that for the instant he forgot the agony of his wound, and thought only of flight.

Flight! He could hardly stand and if he were in full possession of all the best powers of his slight and youthful frame, where could he fly to? He pushed against the garden gate. It was unlocked, and swung open on its hinges.

He tottered across the lawn, climbed the steps, knocked faintly at the door, and his whole strength failing him, sank down against one of the pillars of the little portico.

◆   ◆   ◆

And now what happened to this poor wretched little boy? The door was opened, and he was recognized as one of the daring burglars. He was seized and dragged into the house by the man servant, and a doctor was sent for.

Doctor Losberne was one of the kindest men in the world, and he had Oliver put to bed, and dressed his wound and did everything he could for him. Then afterwards he saw Mrs. Maylie, the lady of the house, and her daughter Rose, to tell them about the dreadful burglar that had broken into the house the night before.

"This is a very extraordinary thing, Mrs. Maylie," said the doctor, standing with his back to the door as if to keep it shut.

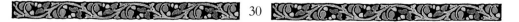

"He is not in danger, I hope?" said the old lady.

"Why, that would not be an extraordinary thing, under the circumstances," replied the doctor, "though I don't think he is. Have you seen this thief?"

"No," rejoined the old lady.

"Nor heard anything about him?"

"No. Rose wished to see the man," said Mrs. Maylie, "but I wouldn't hear of it."

"Humph!" rejoined the doctor. "There's nothing very alarming in his appearance. Have you any objection to see him in my presence?"

"If it be necessary," replied the old lady, "certainly not."

"Then I think it is necessary," said the doctor. "At all events, I am quite sure that you would deeply regret not having done so if you postponed it. He is perfectly quiet and comfortable now. Allow me—Miss Rose, will you permit me? Not the slightest fear, I pledge you my honor."

With many more loquacious assurances that they would be agreeably surprised in the aspect of the criminal, the doctor drew the young lady's arm through one of his, and offering his disengaged hand to Mrs. Maylie, led them with much ceremony and stateliness upstairs.

"Now," said the doctor in a whisper, as he softly turned the handle of a bedroom door, "let us hear what you think of him. He has not been shaved very recently, but he doesn't look at all ferocious, notwithstanding. Stop, though—let me see that he is in visiting order first."

Stepping before them he looked into the room, and, motioning them to advance, closed the door when they had entered, and gently drew back the curtains of the bed.

Upon it, instead of the dogged, black-visaged ruffian they had expected to behold, there lay a mere child, worn with pain and exhaustion, and sunk into a deep sleep.

His wounded arm, bound and splintered up, was crossed upon his breast, and his head reclined upon the other, which was half hidden by his long hair as it streamed over the pillow.

The honest gentleman held the curtain in his hand, and looked on for a minute or so in silence. While he was watching the patient thus, the younger lady glided softly past, and seating herself in a chair by the bedside, gathered Oliver's hair from his face, and as she stooped over him her tears fell upon his forehead.

The boy stirred, and smiled in his sleep, as though these marks of pity and compassion had awakened some pleasant dream of a love and affection he had never known. Thus a strain of gentle music, or the rippling of water in a silent place, or the odor of a flower, or the mention of a familiar word, will sometimes call up sudden dim remembrances of scenes that never were in this life, which vanish like a breath, and which some brief memory of a happier existence, long gone by, would seem to have awakened, for no power of the human mind can ever recall them.

When Oliver awoke he told them all his strange history, but was often compelled to stop by pain and want of strength.

It was a solemn thing to hear, in the darkened room, the feeble voice of the sick child recounting a weary catalogue of evils and calamities which hard men had brought upon him.

Oliver's pillow was smoothed by women's hands that night, and loveliness and virtue watched him as he slept.

And this was the end of the poor boy's troubles. It is a very strange thing to have to relate, but the pretty Rose Maylie turned out to be Oliver's aunt—his mother's own sister! From the moment he entered Mrs. Maylie's house his life was as happy as it had been miserable in the past. From that day forth he saw no more of that fearful place where the thieves lived, and the thieves themselves were caught and sent to prison, and everybody said it served them right.

Jenny Wren

Walking into the city one holiday, a great many years ago, a gentleman ran up the steps of a tall house in the neighborhood of St. Mary Axe. The lower windows were those of a countinghouse, but the blinds, like those of the entire front of the house, were drawn down.

The gentleman knocked and rang several times before anyone came, but at last an old man opened the door. "What were you up to that you did not hear me?" said Mr. Fledgeby irritably.

"I was taking the air at the top of the house, sir," said the old man meekly, "it being a holiday. What might you please to want, sir?"

"Humph! Holiday indeed," grumbled his master, who was a toy merchant among other things. He then seated himself in the countinghouse and gave the old man—Riah by name—directions as to the various business matters about which he had come to speak, and, as he rose to go, exclaimed, "By the bye, how *do* you take the air? Do you stick your head out of a chimney pot?"

"No, sir, I have made a little garden on the leads."

"Let's look at it," said Mr. Fledgeby.

"Sir, I have company there," returned Riah hesitating, "but will you please come up and see them?"

Mr. Fledgeby nodded, and, passing his master with a bow, the old man led the way up flight after flight of stairs, till they arrived at the house top. Seated on a carpet, and leaning against a chimney stack, were two girls bending over books. Some humble creepers were trained around

the chimney pots, and evergreens were placed around the roof, and a few more books, a basket of gaily colored scraps and bits of tinsel, and another of common print stuff, lay near. One of the girls rose on seeing that Riah had brought a visitor, but the other remarked, "I'm the person of the house downstairs, but I can't get up, whoever you are, because my back is bad, and my legs are queer."

"This is my master," said Riah, speaking to the two girls, "and this," he added, turning to Mr. Fledgeby, "is Miss Jenny Wren. She lives in this house, and is a clever little dressmaker for little people. Her friend Lizzie," continued Riah, introducing the second girl. "They are good girls, both, and as busy as they are good. In spare moments they come up here, and take to book learning."

"We are glad to come up here for rest, sir," said Lizzie, with a grateful look at the old man. "This place means so much to us."

"Humph!" said Mr. Fledgeby, looking round, "Humph!" He was so much surprised that apparently he couldn't get beyond that word, and as he went down again the old chimney pots in their black cowls seemed to turn round and look after him as if they were saying "Humph" too.

Lizzie, the elder of these two girls, was strong and handsome, but the little Jenny Wren, whom she so loved and protected, was small and deformed, though she had a beautiful little face, and the longest and loveliest golden hair in the world, which fell about her like a cloak of shining curls, as though to hide the poor little misshapen figure. Old Riah, as well as Lizzie, was always kind and gentle to Jenny Wren, who called him her godfather. She had a father, who shared her poor little rooms, whom she called her child, for he was a bad, drunken, disreputable old man, and the poor girl had to care for him, and earn money to keep them both. She suffered a great deal, for the poor little bent back always ached sadly, and was often weary from incessant work, but it was only on rare occasions, when alone or with her friend Lizzie, who often brought her work and sat in Jenny's room, that the brave child ever complained of her hard lot.

Sometimes the two girls, Jenny helping herself along with a crutch, would go and walk about the fashionable streets, to note how the grand folks were dressed. As they walked along, Jenny would tell her friend of the fancies she had when sitting alone at her work.

"I imagine birds till I can hear them sing," she said one day, "and flowers till I can smell them. And oh! the beautiful children that come to me in the early mornings! They are quite different than other children, not like me, never cold, or anxious, or tired, or hungry, never any pain. They come in numbers, in long bright slanting rows, all dressed in white, and with shiny heads. 'Who is this in pain?' they say, and they sweep around and about me, take me up in their arms, and I feel so light, and all the pain goes. I know when they are coming a long way off, by hearing them say, 'Who is this in pain?' and I answer, 'Oh my blessed children, it's poor me! have pity on me, and take me up and then the pain will go.' "

Lizzie sat stroking and brushing the beautiful hair, while the tired little dressmaker leaned against her when they were at home again, and as she kissed her good night, a miserable old man stumbled into the room. "How's my Jenny Wren, best of children?" he mumbled, as he shuffled unsteadily towards her, but Jenny pointed her small finger towards him exclaiming—"Go along with you, you bad, wicked, old child, you troublesome wicked, old thing. *I* know where you have been. *I* know your tricks and your manners." The wretched man began to whimper, like a scolded child. "Slave, slave, slave, from morning to night," went on Jenny, still shaking her finger at him, "and all for this. Ain't you ashamed of yourself, you disgraceful boy?"

"Yes, my dear, yes," stammered the tipsy old father, tumbling into a corner. Thus was the poor little dolls' dressmaker dragged down day by day by the very hands that should have cared for and held her up.

One day when Jenny was on her way home with Riah, who had accompanied her on one of her expeditions to the West End, they came on a small crowd of people. A tipsy man had been knocked down and badly hurt.

"Let us see what it is!" said Jenny, coming swiftly forward on her crutches. The next moment she exclaimed, "Oh, gentlemen—gentlemen, he is my child, he belongs to me, my poor, bad, old child!"

"Your child—belongs to you—" repeated the man who was about to lift the helpless figure onto a stretcher, which had been brought for the purpose. "Aye, it's old Dolls—tipsy old Dolls—" cried someone in the crowd, for it was by this name that they knew the old man.

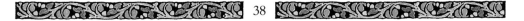

"He's her father, sir," said Riah in a low tone to the doctor, who was now bending over the stretcher.

"So much the worse," answered the doctor, "for the man is dead."

Yes, Mr. Dolls was dead, and many were the dresses which the weary fingers of the sorrowful little worker must make to pay for his humble funeral, and buy a black frock for herself. Riah sat by her in her poor room, saying a word of comfort now and then, and Lizzie came and went, and did all manner of little things to help her; but often the tears rolled down onto her work. "My poor child," she said to Riah, "my poor old child, and to think I scolded him so."

"You were always a good, brave, patient girl," returned Riah, smiling a little over her quaint fancy about her *child,* "always good and patient, however tired."

And so the poor little "person of the house" was left alone but for the faithful affection of the kind old man, and her friend Lizzie. Her room grew pretty and comfortable, for she was in great request in her "profession" as she called it, and there was now no one to spend and waste her earnings.

Tiny Tim

It will surprise you all very much to hear that there was once a man who did not like Christmas. In fact, he had been heard on several occasions to use the word *humbug* with regard to it. His name was Scrooge, and he was a hard, sour-tempered man of business, intent only on saving and making money, and caring nothing for anyone. He paid the poor, hard-working clerk in his office as little as he could possibly get the work done for, and lived on as little as possible himself, alone, in two dismal rooms. He was never merry or comfortable, or happy, and he hated other people to be so, and that was the reason why he hated Christmas, because people *will* be happy at Christmas, if they possibly can, and like to have a little money to make themselves and others comfortable.

Well, it was Christmas Eve, a very cold and foggy one, and Mr. Scrooge, having given his poor clerk unwilling permission to spend Christmas Day at home, locked up his office and went home himself in a very bad temper, and with a cold in his head. After having taken some gruel as he sat over a miserable fire in his dismal room, he got into bed, and had some wonderful and disagreeable dreams, to which we will leave him, while we see how Tiny Tim, the son of his poor clerk, spent Christmas Day.

The name of this clerk was Bob Crachit. He had a wife and five other children besides Tim, who was weak and delicate. His legs were crippled. He was a dear little boy too, gentle and patient and loving, with a sweet

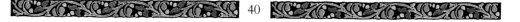

face of his own, which no one could help looking at, and he was dearly loved by his father, and the rest of his family.

Whenever he could spare the time, it was Mr. Crachit's delight to carry his little boy out on his shoulder to see the shops and the people. Today he had taken him to church for the first time.

"Whatever has got your precious father, and your brother Tiny Tim!" exclaimed Mrs. Crachit. "Here's dinner all ready to be dished up. I've never known him so late on Christmas Day before."

"Here he is, Mother!" cried Belinda, and "Here he is!" cried the other children as Mr. Crachit came in, his long comforter hanging three feet from under his threadbare coat; for cold as it was, the poor clerk had no topcoat. Tiny Tim was perched on his father's shoulder with his little crutch in his hand.

"And how did Tim behave?" asked Mrs. Crachit.

"As good as gold and better," replied the father. "I think, Wife, the child gets thoughtful, sitting at home so much. He told me, coming home, that he hoped the people in church who saw he was crippled would be pleased to remember on Christmas Day who it was who made the lame to walk."

"Bless his sweet heart!" said his mother in a

trembling voice, and the father's voice trembled too, as he remarked that "Tiny Tim is growing strong and hearty at last."

Dinner was waiting to be dished up. Mrs. Crachit proudly placed a goose upon the table. Belinda brought in the apple sauce, and Peter the mashed potatoes. The other children set chairs, Tim's, as usual, close to his father's. And Tim was so excited that he rapped the table with his knife and cried, "Hurrah!"

After the goose came the pudding, with a great smell of steam, like washing day, as it came out of the copper. In it came, all a-blaze, with its

sprig of holly in the middle, and was eaten to the last morsel. Then apples and oranges were set upon the table, and a shovelful of chestnuts on the fire, and Mr. Crachit served round some hot sweet stuff out of a jug as they closed round the fire, and said, "A Merry Christmas to us all, my dears, God bless us."

"God bless us, every one," echoed Tiny Tim, and then they drank each other's health, and Mr. Scrooge's health, and told stories and sang songs. Tim, who had a sweet little voice, sang, very well indeed, a song about a child who was lost in the snow on Christmas Day.

Now I told you that Mr. Scrooge had some disagreeable and wonderful dreams on Christmas Eve, and so he had. In one of them he dreamt that a Christmas spirit showed him his clerk's home. He saw them all gathered round the fire, and heard them drink his health, and Tiny Tim's song, and he took special note of Tiny Tim himself.

In his dreams that night Scrooge visited all sorts of places and saw all sorts of people, for different spirits came to him and led him about where they would, and presently he was taken again to his poor clerk's home. The mother was doing some needlework, seated by the table. A tear dropped on it now and then, and she said, poor thing, that the work, which was black, hurt her eyes. The children sat, sad and silent, about the room, except Tiny Tim, who was not there. Upstairs the father, with his face hidden in his hands, sat beside a little bed, on which lay a tiny figure, white and still.

"My little child, my pretty little child," he sobbed, as the tears fell through his fingers on to the floor.

"Tiny Tim died because his father was too poor to give him what was necessary to make him well; *you* kept him poor," said the dream spirit to Mr. Scrooge.

The father kissed the cold, little face on the bed, and went downstairs, where the sprays of holly still remained about the humble room; and, taking his hat, went out, with a wistful glance at the little crutch in the corner as he shut the door.

Mr. Scrooge saw all this, and many more things as strange and sad—the spirit took care of that. But, wonderful to relate, he woke next morning feeling a different man—feeling as he had never felt in his life before.

"Why, I am as light as a feather, and as happy as an angel, and as merry as a schoolboy," he said to himself. "A Merry Christmas to everybody! A Happy New Year to all the world." And a few minutes later he was ordering a turkey to be taken round to Tiny Tim's house, a turkey so large that the man who took it had to go in a cab.

Next morning poor Bob Crachit crept into the office a few minutes

late, expecting to be roundly abused and scolded for it. He soon found, however, that his master was a very different man than the one who had grudged him his Christmas holiday, for there was Scrooge telling him heartily he was going to raise his salary and asking quite affectionately after Tiny Tim! "And mind you make up a good fire in your room before you set to work, Bob," he said, as he closed his own door.

Bob could hardly believe his eyes and ears, but it was all true, and more prosperous times came to his family, and happier, for Tiny Tim did not die—not a bit of it. Mr. Scrooge was a second father to him from that day. He wanted for nothing, and grew up strong and hearty. Mr. Scrooge loved him, and well he might, for was it not Tiny Tim who had unconsciously, through the Christmas dream spirit, touched his hard heart, and caused him to be a good and happy man.

Little David Copperfield

Little David Copperfield lived with his mother in a pretty house in the village of Blunderstone in Suffolk. He had never known his father, who died before David could remember anything, and he had neither brothers nor sisters. He was fondly loved by his pretty young mother and their kind, good servant Peggotty, and David was a very happy little fellow. They had very few friends, and the only relation Mrs. Copperfield talked about was an aunt of David's father, a tall and rather terrible old lady, from all accounts, who had once been to see them when David was quite a tiny baby, and had been so angry to find David was not a little girl, that she had left the house quite offended, and had never been heard of since. One visitor, a tall dark gentleman, David did not like at all, and he was rather inclined to be jealous that his mother should be friendly with the stranger.

One day Peggotty, the servant, asked David if he would like to go with her on a visit to her brother at Yarmouth.

"Is your brother an agreeable man, Peggotty?" he inquired.

"Oh, what an agreeable man he is!" cried Peggotty. "Then there's the sea, and the boats and ships, and the fishermen, and the beach. And 'Am to play with."

Ham was her nephew. David was quite anxious to go when he heard of all these delights, but what would his mother do all alone? Peggotty told him his mother was going to pay a visit to some friends, and would be sure to let him go. So all was arranged, and they were to start the next

47

day in the carrier's cart. David was so eager that he wanted to put his hat and coat on the night before! But when the time came to say good-bye to his dear mamma, he cried a little, for he had never left her before.

It was rather a slow way of traveling, and poor David was very tired and sleepy when they arrived at Yarmouth, and found Ham waiting to meet them. He was a great strong fellow, six feet high, and took David on his back and the box under his arm to carry both to the house.

David was delighted to find that this house was made of a real big black boat, with a door and windows cut in the side, and an iron funnel sticking out of the roof for a chimney. Inside, it was very cozy and clean, and David had a tiny bedroom in the stern. He was much pleased to find a dear little girl, about his own age, to play with, and soon discovered that she and Ham were orphans, children of Mr. Peggotty's brother and sister, whose fathers had both been drowned at sea, so kind Mr. Peggotty had taken them to live with him. An elderly woman, named Mrs. Gummidge, lived with them too, and did the cooking and cleaning, for she was a poor widow and had no home of her own. David thought Mr. Peggotty was very good to take all these people to live with him, and he was quite right, for Mr. Peggotty was only a poor man himself and had to work hard to get a living. David was very happy in this queer house, playing on the beach with Em'ly, as they called the little girl. He told her all about his happy home, and she told him how her father had been drowned at sea before she came to live with her uncle.

David said he thought Mr. Peggotty must be a very good man.

"Good!" said Em'ly. "If ever I was to be a lady, I'd give him a sky-blue coat with diamond buttons, nankeen trousers, a red velvet waistcoat, a cocked hat, a large gold watch, a silver pipe, and a box of money!"

David was quite sorry to leave these kind people and his dear little companion, but still he was glad to think he should get back to his own dear mamma. When he reached home, however, he found a great change. His mother was married to the dark man David did not like, whose name was Mr. Murdstone. He was a stern, hard man, who had no love for little

David and did not allow his mother to pet and indulge him as she had done before. Mr. Murdstone's sister came to live with them, and as she was even more difficult to please than her brother, and disliked boys, David's life was no longer a happy one. He tried to be good and obedient, for he knew it made his mother very unhappy to see him punished and found fault with. He had always had lessons with his mother, and as she was patient and gentle, he had enjoyed learning to read, but now he had a great many very hard lessons to do, and was so frightened and shy when Mr. and Miss Murdstone were in the room, that he did not get on at all well, and was continually in disgrace. His only pleasure was to go up into a little room at the top of the house where he had found a number of books that had belonged to his own father, and he would sit and read *Robinson Crusoe*, and many tales of travels and adventures, and he imagined himself to be the heroes, and went about for days with the center-piece out of an old set of boot trees, pretending to be a captain in the British Royal Navy.

But one day he got into sad trouble over his lessons, and Mr. Murdstone was very angry, and took him away from his mother and beat him with a cane. David had never been beaten in his life before, and was so maddened by the pain and by rage that he bit Mr. Murdstone's hand! Now, indeed, he had done something to deserve the punishment, and Mr. Murdstone, in a fury, beat him savagely, and left him sobbing and crying on the floor, with a dreadful feeling in his heart of how wicked and full of hate he was. David was kept locked up in his room for some days, seeing no one but Miss Murdstone, who brought him his food. At last, one night, he heard his name whispered at the keyhole.

"Is that you, Peggotty?" he asked, groping his way to the door.

"Yes, my Davy. Be as soft as a mouse or the cat will hear us."

David understood she meant Miss Murdstone, whose room was quite near. "How's Mamma, Peggotty dear? Is she very angry with me?" he whispered. Peggotty was crying softly on her side of the door as David was on his.

"No—not very," she said.

"What is going to be done with me, dear Peggotty, do you know?" asked poor David, who had been wondering all these long, lonely days.

"School—near London—"

"When, Peggotty?"

"Tomorrow," answered Peggotty.

"Shan't I see Mamma?"

"Yes—morning," she said, and went on to promise David she would always love him, and take the greatest care of his dear mamma, and write to him every week.

"Thank you, thank you, dear Peggotty, and do write and tell Mr. Peggotty, and Em'ly and Ham and Mrs. Gummidge, that I am not so bad as they might suppose, and give them all my love. Will you, please, Peggotty?"

Peggotty promised, and they both kissed the keyhole most tenderly, and parted.

The next morning David saw his mother, very pale and with red eyes. He ran to her arms and begged her to forgive him.

"Oh, Davy," she said, "that you should hurt anyone I love! I forgive you Davy, but it grieves me so that you should have such bad passions in your heart. Try to be better, pray to be better."

David was very unhappy that his mother should think him so wicked, and though she kissed him and said, "I forgive you, my dear boy, God bless you," he cried so bitterly when he was on his way in the carrier's cart, that his pocket handkerchief had to be spread out on the horse's back to dry.

After they had gone a little way the cart stopped, and Peggotty came running up with a parcel of cakes and a purse for David. After giving him a good hug, she ran off.

David found three bright shillings in the purse, and two half-crowns wrapped in paper on which was written, in his mother's hand—"For Davy. With my love."

David shared his cakes with the carrier, who asked if Peggotty made them, and David told him yes, she did all their cooking. The carrier looked thoughtful, and then asked David if he would send a message to Peggotty from him. David agreed, and the message was "Barkis is willing." While David was waiting for the coach at Yarmouth, he wrote to Peggotty.

"My Dear Peggotty,—I have come here safe. Barkis is willing. My love to Mamma.—Yours affectionately.

"P.S.—He says he particularly wanted you to know *Barkis is willing.*"

At Yarmouth he found dinner was ordered for him, and felt very shy at having a table all to himself, and very much alarmed when the waiter told him he had seen a gentleman fall down dead after drinking some of their beer. David said he would have some water, and was quite grateful

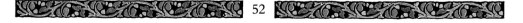

to the waiter for drinking the ale that had been ordered for him, for fear the people of the hotel should be offended. The waiter also helped David to eat his dinner, and accepted one of his bright shillings.

After a long, tiring journey by the coach, for there were no trains in those days, David arrived in London and was taken by one of the masters, Mr. Mell, to a school at Blackheath.

When they got to Salem House, as the school was called, David found the holidays were not over, but that he had been sent before the school was opened as a punishment for his wickedness, and was also to wear a placard on his back, on which was written—"Take care of him. He bites." This made David miserable, and he dreaded the return of the boys. Fortunately for David, the first boy who came back, Tommy Traddles, was not an unkind boy, and seemed to think the placard rather a joke, and showed it to all the boys as they came back, with the remark—"Look here—here's a game!"

Some of the boys teased David by pretending he was a dog, calling him Towser, and patting and stroking him. But, on the whole, it was not so bad as David had expected. The head boy, too, Steerforth, who was very handsome and some years older than David, said he thought it was "a jolly shame" when he heard all about David's punishment, which consoled the little boy very much. Steerforth promised to take care of him, and David loved him dearly, and thought him a great hero. Steerforth took a great fancy to the pretty, bright-eyed little fellow, and David became a favorite with all the boys, by telling them all he could remember of the tales he had read. He spent all his money the first day on a grand supper in their bedroom (on Steerforth's advice), and heard many things about the school, and how severe Mr. Creakle, the headmaster, was. This he found was very true, and the boys were always being caned and punished, especially poor Traddles, who often suffered from his firmly refusing ever to betray any of his schoolfellows.

One day David had a visit from Mr. Peggotty and Ham, who brought two enormous lobsters, a huge crab, and a large canvas bag of shrimps, as they "remembered he was partial to a relish with his meals."

David was proud to introduce his friend Steerforth to these kind, simple friends, and told them how good Steerforth was to him, and how he helped him with his work and took care of him. Steerforth delighted the fishermen with his friendly, pleasant manners.

The "relish" was much appreciated by the boys at supper that night. Only poor Traddles became very ill from eating crab so late.

At last the holidays came, and David went home. The carrier, Barkis, met him at Yarmouth, and was rather gruff, which David soon found out was because he had not had any answer to his message. David promised to ask Peggotty for one.

When he got home David found he had a little baby brother, and his mother and Peggotty were very much pleased to see him again. They had a very happy afternoon the day he came. Mr. and Miss Murdstone were out, and David sat with his mother and Peggotty, and told them all about his school and Steerforth, and took the little baby in his arms and held it lovingly. But when the Murdstones came back David was more unhappy than ever, for they showed plainly they disliked him, and thought him in the way, and scolded him, and would not allow him to touch the baby, or even to sit with Peggotty in the kitchen. He was not sorry when the time came for him to go back to school, except for leaving his dear mamma and the baby. She kissed him very tenderly at parting, and held up the baby for him to see as he drove off in the carrier's cart once more.

About two months after he had been back at school he was sent for one day to go into the parlor. He hurried in joyfully, for it was his birthday, and he thought it might be a hamper from Peggotty. But, alas! no. It was very sad news Mrs. Creakle had to give him. His dear mamma

had died! Mrs. Creakle was very kind and gentle to the desolate little boy, and the boys, especially Traddles, were very sorry for him.

David went home the next day, and heard that the dear baby had died too. Peggotty received him with great tenderness, and told him about his mother's illness and how she had sent him a loving message.

"Tell my dearest boy that his mother, as she lay here, blessed him not once, but a thousand times," and she had prayed to God to protect and keep her fatherless boy.

Mr. Murdstone did not take any notice of poor little David, nor had Miss Murdstone a word of kindness for the orphan. Peggotty was to leave in a month, and, to their great joy, David was allowed to go with her on a visit to Mr. Peggotty. On their way David found out that the mysterious message he had given to Peggotty meant that Barkis wanted to marry her, and Peggotty had consented. Everyone in Mr. Peggotty's cottage was pleased to see David, and did their best to comfort him. Little Em'ly was at school when he arrived, and he went out to meet her. But when he saw her coming along, her blue eyes bluer, and her bright face prettier than ever, he pretended not to know her, and was passing by, when Em'ly laughed and ran away. So, of course, he was obliged to run and catch her, and try to kiss her, but she would not let him, saying she was not a baby now. But she was kind to him all the same, and when they spoke about the loss of his dear mother, David saw that her eyes were full of tears.

"Ah," said Mr. Peggotty, running his fingers through her bright curls, "here's another orphan, you see, sir, and here," giving Ham a backhanded knock in the chest, "is another of 'em, though he don't look much like it."

"If I had *you* for a guardian, Mr. Peggotty," said David, "I don't think I should *feel* much like it."

"Well said, Master Davy, bor!" cried Ham, delighted. "Hoorah, well said! No more you wouldn't, bor, bor!" returning Mr. Peggotty's backhander, while little Em'ly got up and kissed her uncle.

During this visit Peggotty was married to Mr. Barkis, and had a nice little house of her own, and David spent the night in a little room in the roof before he was to return home.

"Young or old, Davy dear, so long as I have this house over my

head," said Peggotty, "you shall find it as if I expected you here directly every minute. I shall keep it as I used to keep your old little room, my darling. And if you was to go to China, you might think of its being kept just the same all the time you were away."

David felt how good and true a friend she was, and thanked her as well as he could, for they had brought him to the gate of his home, and Peggotty had him clasped in her arms.

Poor little lonely David, with no one near to speak a loving word, or a face to look on his with love and liking, only the two persons who had broken his mother's heart to live with. How utterly wretched and forlorn he felt! He found he was not to go back to school any more, and wandered about sad and solitary, neglected and uncared for. Peggotty's weekly visits were his only comfort. He longed to go to school, however hard it might be, to be taught something anyhow, anywhere. But no one took any pains with him, and he had no friends near who could help him.

At last one day, after some weary months had passed, Mr. Murdstone told him he was to go to London and earn his own living. There was a place for him at Murdstone & Grinby's, a firm in the wine trade. His lodging and clothes would be provided for him by his stepfather, and he would earn enough for his food and pocket money.

The next day David was sent up to London with the manager, dressed in a shabby little white hat, with black crepe round it for his mourning for his mother, a black jacket, and hard, stiff corduroy trousers—a little fellow of ten years old to fight his own battles with the world!

His place, he found, was one of the lowest in the firm of Murdstone & Grinby, with boys of no education and in quite an inferior station to himself. His duties were to wash the bottles, stick on labels, and do other menial chores. David was utterly miserable at being degraded in this way, when he thought of his former companions, Steerforth and Traddles, and his hopes of becoming a learned and distinguished man. He shed bitter tears, because he feared he would forget all he had learned at school.

His lodging, one bare little room, was in the house of some people named Micawber, shiftless, careless, good-natured people, who were always in debt and difficulties. David felt great pity for their misfortunes and did what he could to help poor Mrs. Micawber to sell her books and other little things she could spare, to buy food for herself, her husband, and their four children. David was too young and childish to know how to provide properly for himself, and often found he was obliged to live on bread and slices of cold pudding at the end of the week. If he had not been a very innocent, good little boy, he might easily have fallen into bad ways at this time. The dear little unselfish fellow would not even tell Peggotty how miserable he was, for fear of distressing her.

The troubles of the Micawbers increased more and more, until at last they were obliged to leave London. David was very sad, for he had been with them so long that he felt they were his friends, and the prospect of being once more utterly alone, and having to find a lodging with strangers, made him so unhappy that he determined to endure this kind of life no longer. The last Sunday the Micawbers were in town he dined with them. He had bought a spotted horse for their little boy, a doll for the little girl, and had saved up a shilling for the poor servant girl.

After he had seen them off the next morning by the coach, he wrote to Peggotty to ask her if she knew where his aunt, Miss Betsey Trotwood, lived, and to borrow half a guinea. He had resolved to run away from Murdstone and Grinby's, and go to his aunt and tell her his story. He remembered his mother telling him of her visit when he was a baby, and that she fancied Miss Betsey had stroked her hair gently. This gave him courage to appeal to her. Peggotty wrote, enclosing the half-guinea, and saying she only knew Miss Trotwood lived near Dover, but whether in that place itself, or at Folkestone, Sandgate, or Hythe, she could not tell. Hearing that all these places were close together, David made up his mind to start.

Since he had received his week's wages in advance, he waited till the following Saturday, thinking it would not be honest to go before. He

went out to look for someone to carry his box to the coach office, and unfortunately employed a wicked young man who not only ran off with the box, but robbed him of his half-guinea, leaving poor David in dire distress. In despair, he started off to walk to Dover, and was forced to sell his waistcoat to buy some bread. The first night he found his way to his old school at Blackheath, and slept on a haystack close by, feeling some comfort in the thought of the boys being near. He knew Steerforth had left, or he would have tried to see him.

On he trudged the next day and sold his jacket at Chatham to a dreadful old man, who kept him waiting all day for the money, which was only one shilling and fourpence. He was afraid to buy anything but bread or to spend any money on a bed or a shelter for the night. He was terribly frightened by some rough tramps, who threw stones at him when he did not answer to their calls.

After six days, he arrived at Dover, ragged, dusty, and half-dead with hunger and fatigue. But here, at first, he could get no tidings of his aunt, and, in despair, was going to try some of the other places Peggotty had mentioned, when the driver of a fly dropped his horsecloth, and as David was handing it up to him, he saw something kind in the man's face that encouraged him to ask once more if he knew where Miss Trotwood lived.

The man directed him towards some houses on the heights, and there David went. Going into a little shop, he by chance met with Miss Trotwood's maid, who showed him the house, and went in leaving him standing at the gate, a forlorn little creature, without a jacket or waistcoat, his white hat crushed out of shape, his shoes worn out, his shirt and trousers torn and stained, his pretty curly hair tangled, his face and hands sunburned and covered with dust. Lifting his big, wistful eyes to one of the windows above, he saw a pleasant-faced gentleman with gray hair, who nodded at him several times, then shook his head and went away.

David was just turning away to think what he should do, when a tall, erect, elderly lady, with a gardening apron on and a knife in her hand,

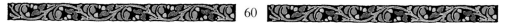

came out of the house, and began to dig up a root in the garden.

"Go away," she said. "Go away. No boys here."

But David felt desperate. Going in softly, he stood beside her, and touched her with his finger, and said timidly, "If you please, ma'am—" and when she looked up, he went on, "Please, Aunt, I am your nephew."

"Oh, Lord!" she exclaimed in astonishment, and sat flat down on the path, staring at him, while he continued.

"I am David Copperfield of Blunderstone, in Suffolk, where you came the night I was born, and saw my dear mamma. I have been very unhappy since she died. I have been slighted and taught nothing, and thrown upon myself, and put to work not fit for me. It made me run away to you. I was robbed at first starting out and have walked all the way, and have never slept in a bed since I began the journey." Here he broke into a passion of crying. His aunt jumped up and took him into the house, where she opened a cupboard and took out some bottles, pouring some of the contents of each into his mouth, not noticing in her agitation what they were, for David fancied he tasted aniseed water, anchovy sauce, and salad dressing! Then she put him on the sofa and sent Janet, the servant, to ask "Mr. Dick" to come down.

The gentleman whom David had seen at the window came in and was told by Miss Trotwood who the ragged little object on the sofa was, and she finished by saying, "Now here you see young David Copperfield, and the question is, What shall I do with him?"

"Do with him?" answered Mr. Dick. Then, after some consideration, and looking at David, he said, "Why, if I was you, I should wash him!"

Miss Trotwood was quite pleased at this, and a warm bath was got ready at once, after which David was dressed in a shirt and trousers belonging to Mr. Dick (for Janet had burned his rags), rolled up in several shawls, and put on the sofa till dinner time. There he slept, and woke with the impression that his aunt had come and smoothed his hair off his face, and murmured, "Pretty fellow, poor fellow."

After dinner he had to tell his story all over again to his aunt and Mr. Dick. Miss Trotwood again asked Mr. Dick's advice, and was delighted when that gentleman suggested he should be put to bed.

David knelt down to say his prayers that night in a pleasant room facing the sea, and as he lay in the clean, snow-white bed, he felt so grateful and comforted that he prayed earnestly he might never be homeless again, and might never forget the homeless.

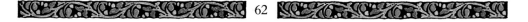

The next morning his aunt told him she had written to Mr. Murdstone. David was alarmed to think that his stepfather knew where he was,
and exclaimed, "Oh, I don't know what I shall do if I have to go back to
Mr. Murdstone!"

But his aunt said nothing of her intentions, and David was uncertain
what was to become of him. He hoped she might befriend him.

At last Mr. and Miss Murdstone arrived. To Miss Betsey's great
indignation, Miss Murdstone rode a donkey across the green in front of
the house, and stopped at the gate. Nothing made Miss Trotwood so
angry as to see donkeys on that green, and David had already seen several
battles between his aunt or Janet and the donkey boys.

After driving away the donkey and the boy who had dared to bring
it here, Miss Trotwood received her visitors. David she kept near her,
fenced in with a chair.

Mr. Murdstone told Miss Betsey that David was a very bad, stub-
born, violent-tempered boy, whom he had tried to improve, but could
not succeed; that he had put him in a respectable business from which he
had run away. If Miss Trotwood chose to protect and encourage him
now, she must do it always, for he had come to fetch him away there and
then, and if he was not ready to come, and Miss Trotwood did not wish
to give him up to be dealt with exactly as Mr. Murdstone liked, he would
cast him off for always, and have no more to do with him.

"Are you ready to go, David?" asked his aunt.

But David answered no, and begged and prayed her for his father's
sake to befriend and protect him, for neither Mr. nor Miss Murdstone had
ever liked him or been kind to him, and had made his mamma, who
always loved him dearly, very unhappy about him, and he had been very
miserable.

"Mr. Dick," said Miss Trotwood, "what shall I do with this child?"

Mr. Dick considered. "Have him measured for a suit of clothes
directly."

"Mr. Dick," said Miss Trotwood, "your advice is invaluable."

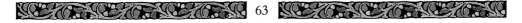

Then she pulled David towards her, and said to Mr. Murdstone, "You can go when you like. I'll take my chance with the boy. If he's all you say he is I can at least do as much for him as you have done. But I don't believe a word of it."

Then she told Mr. Murdstone what she thought of the way he had treated David and his mother, which did not make that gentleman feel very comfortable, and finished by turning to Miss Murdstone, and saying, "Good day to you, too, ma'am, and if I ever see you ride a donkey across my green again, as sure as you have a head upon your shoulders, I'll knock your bonnet off and tread upon it!"

This startled Miss Murdstone so much that she went off quite quietly with her brother, while David, overjoyed, threw his arms round his aunt's neck, and kissed and thanked her with great heartiness.

Some clothes were bought for him and marked "Trotwood Copperfield," for his aunt wished to call him by her name.

Now David felt his troubles were over, and he began quite a new life, well cared for and kindly treated. He was sent to a very nice school in Canterbury, where his aunt left him with these words, which David never forgot.

"Trot, be a credit to yourself and me, and Mr. Dick, and Heaven be with you. Never be mean in anything, never be false, never be cruel. Avoid these three vices, Trot, and I shall always be hopeful of you."

David did his best to show his gratitude to his dear aunt by studying hard, and trying to be all she could wish.

The Blind Toymaker

Caleb Plummer and his daughter, who was blind, lived alone in a little cracked nutshell of a house. They were toymakers, and their house, which was so small that it might have been knocked to pieces with a hammer, and carried away in a cart, was stuck like a toadstool onto the premises of Messrs. Gruff & Tackleton, the toy merchants for whom they worked, the latter of whom was himself both Gruff and Tackleton in one.

Actually, only Caleb lived here. His daughter lived in an enchanted palace, which her father's love had created for her. She did not know that the ceilings were cracked, the plaster tumbling down, and the woodwork rotten. She did not know that everything about her was old and ugly and poverty-stricken, and that her father was a gray-haired stooping old man, and that the master for whom they worked was a hard and brutal task-master—oh, dear no, she fancied a pretty, cozy, compact little home full of tokens of a kind master's care, a smart, brisk, gallant-looking father, and a handsome and noble-looking toy merchant who was an angel of goodness.

This was all Caleb's doing. When his daughter was a baby he had determined, in his great love and sympathy for her, that her deprivation should be turned into a blessing, and her life should be as happy as he could make it. And she was happy. Everything about her she saw with her father's eyes, in the rainbow-colored light with which it was his care and pleasure to invest it.

65

A strange home it was. Their living room was also their workroom. On shelves around it were stored dolls' houses of all sizes and descriptions, dolls' furniture, and dolls themselves of all ranks of life, from the penny plebeian Dutch to the aristocratic wax beauty. There was also a quantity of gay material, out of which Bertha, the blind girl, made dolls' garments. There were piles and rows of Noah's arks, carts and horses, fiddles, drums, and tumblers, and in the midst of it all Bertha sat busily at work, making a doll's frock, while Caleb bent over the opposite side of the table painting a doll's house.

"You were out in the rain last night in your beautiful new great-coat," said Bertha.

"Yes, in my beautiful new greatcoat," answered Caleb, glancing to where a roughly made garment of sackcloth was hung up to dry.

"How glad I am you bought it, Father."

"And of such a tailor! Quite a fashionable tailor, a bright blue cloth, with bright buttons. It's too good a coat for me."

"Too good!" cried the blind girl, stopping to laugh and clap her hands. "As if anything was too good for my handsome father, with his smiling face, and black hair, and his straight figure, as if *any* thing could be too good for my handsome father."

Ah, if poor Bertha could have seen him, with his wasted, stooping body and worn face, bending wearily over his work in the squalid little room, the sight might have broken her heart.

Caleb began to sing a rollicking song about a sparkling bowl, which made him appear more careworn and poverty-stricken still. "What, you are singing, are you?" growled a gruff voice, as Mr. Tackleton put his head in at the door. "*I* can't afford to sing. I hope you can afford to work too. Hardly time for both, I should say."

"You don't see how the master is winking at me," whispered Caleb in his daughter's ear. "Such a joke, pretending to scold, you know."

The blind girl laughed and nodded, and taking Mr. Tackleton's reluctant hand, kissed it gently. "What is the idiot doing?" grumbled the

toy merchant, pulling his hand roughly away.

"I am thanking you for the little tree, the beautiful little tree," replied Bertha, bringing forward a tiny rose tree in bloom, which, by an innocent deception, Caleb had made her believe was her master's gift, though he himself had gone without a meal or two to buy it.

"Here's bedlam broke loose. What does the idiot mean?" snarled Mr. Tackleton, and giving Caleb some rough orders, he departed without the politeness of a farewell.

"If you could only have seen him winking at me all the time, pretending to be so rough to escape thanking," exclaimed Caleb, when the door was shut.

"Always the same," murmured Bertha to herself, "always the same, refusing to be thanked for his thoughtful and generous gifts, always merry and lighthearted in his desire to amuse me when he comes here."

Now a very sad and curious thing had happened. Caleb in his love for Bertha had so successfully deceived her as to the real character of Mr. Tackleton, making him out to be everything that was noble and good, and full of thought and care for her, that she had fallen in love, not with her master, but with what she imagined him to be, and was happy in an innocent belief in his affection for her. But one day she was told that he

was going to be married, and could not hide from her father the pain and bewilderment she felt at the news.

"Great Heaven!" exclaimed he, when he understood the truth. "Have I deceived you, my poor Bertha, from your cradle, only to break your heart at last." The poor old man went on blaming himself until he hardly knew what to do or where to turn for the distress of mind he had caused her. But he felt he must now tell her the truth.

"Bertha, my dear," said Caleb at length, "I have a confession to make to you—there is something on my mind. Hear me kindly though I have been cruel to you."

"You cruel to me!" cried Bertha, turning her sightless face towards him.

"Not meaning it, my child! Oh, not meaning it! And I never suspected it till the other day. My poor one, my dear blind daughter, the eyes you trusted have been false to you. The world you live in does not exist as I have painted it. I have concealed things from you which would have given you pain. I have invented things to please you, and have surrounded you with fancies."

"But living people are not fancies, Father, you cannot change them."

"I have done so, my child, God forgive me! I have done so! Bertha, the man who is to be married today is in every way unlike what I have described him. He is a hard master to us both, ugly in his looks and in his nature, and hard and heartless as he can be."

"Oh, Heavens! How blind I have been, how could you, Father, and I so helpless!" Poor Caleb hung his head. "Answer me, Father," said Bertha. "What is my home like?"

"A poor place, Bertha, a very poor and bare place! indeed as little able to keep out wind and weather as my sackcloth coat."

"And the presents that I took such care of, that came at my wish, and were so dearly welcome?" Caleb did not answer. "I see, I understand," said Bertha. "And now I am looking at you, at my kind, loving, compassionate father, tell me what he is like?"

"An old man, my child, thin, bent, gray-haired, worn out with hard work and sorrow, a weak, foolish, deceitful old man."

The girl threw herself on her knees before him, and took his gray head in her arms. "It is my sight, it is my sight restored," she cried. "I have been blind, but now I see, I have never till now truly seen my father. Does he think that there is a gallant, handsome father in this earth that I could love so dearly, cherish so devotedly, as this worn and gray-headed old man? Father, there is not a gray hair on your head that shall be forgotten in my prayers and thanks to Heaven."

"My Bertha!" sobbed Caleb, "and the brisk, smart father in the blue coat—he's gone, my child."

"Dearest Father, no, he's not gone, nothing is gone, everything I loved and believed in is here in this worn, old father of mine, and more—oh, so much more, too! I have been happy and contented, but I shall be happier and more contented still, now that I know what you are. I am *not* blind, Father, any longer."

Little Paul Dombey

Little Dombey was the son of a rich city merchant. Ever since his marriage, ten years before this story commences, Mr. Dombey had ardently desired to have a son. He was a cold, stern, and pompous man, whose life and interests were entirely absorbed in his business, which appeared to him to be the most important thing in the whole world. It was not so much that he wanted a son to love, and to love him, but because he was so desirous of having one to associate with himself in the business, and make the house once more Dombey and Son in fact, as it was in name, that the little boy who was born to him was so precious, and so eagerly welcomed.

There was a pretty little girl of six years old, but her father had taken so little notice of her that it was doubtful if he would have known her had he met her in the street. Of what use was a girl to Dombey and Son? She could not go into the business.

Little Dombey's mother died when he was born, but the event did not greatly disturb Mr. Dombey. And since his son lived, what did it matter to him that his little daughter Florence was breaking her heart in loneliness for the mother who had loved and cherished her!

During the first few months of his life, little Dombey grew and flourished. And as soon as he was old enough to take notice, there was no one he loved so well as his sister Florence. He would laugh and hold out his arms as soon as she came in sight, and the affection of her baby brother comforted the lonely little girl, who was never weary of waiting on and playing with him.

72

In due time the baby was taken to church, and was given the name of Paul, his father's name. A grand and stately christening it was, followed by a grand and stately feast. And little Paul, when he was brought in to be admired by the company, was declared by his godmother to be "an angel, and the perfect picture of his own papa."

Whether baby Paul caught cold on his christening day or not, no one could tell, but from that time he seemed to waste and pine. His healthy and thriving babyhood had received a check, and as for illnesses, "There never was a blessed dear so put upon," his nurse said. Every tooth had cost him a fit, and as for chicken pox, whooping cough, and measles, they followed one upon the other and, to quote Nurse Richards again, "seized and worried him like tiger cats," so that by the time he was five years old, though he had the prettiest, sweetest little face in the world, there was always a patient, wistful look upon it, and he was thin and tiny and delicate. He would be as merry and full of spirits as other children when playing with Florence in their nursery, but he soon got tired, and had such old-fashioned ways of speaking and doing things, that Richards often shook her head sadly over him.

When he sat in his little armchair, with his father after dinner, as Mr. Dombey would have him do every day, they were a strange pair—so like, and so unlike each other.

"What is money, Papa?" asked Paul on one of these occasions, crossing his tiny arms as well as he could—just as his father's were crossed.

"Why, gold, silver, and copper. You know what it is well enough, Paul," answered his father.

"Oh yes. I mean, what can money do?"

"Anything, everything—almost," replied Mr. Dombey, taking one of his son's little hands, and beating it softly against his own.

Paul drew his hand gently away. "It didn't save me my mamma, and it can't make me strong and big," said he.

"Why, you *are* strong and big, as big as such little people usually are," returned Mr. Dombey.

73

"No," replied Paul, sighing. "When Florence was as little as me, she was strong and tall, and did not get tired of playing as I do. I am *so* tired sometimes, Papa."

Mr. Dombey's anxiety was aroused, and he summoned his sister, Mrs. Chick, to consult with him over Paul, and the doctor was sent for to examine him.

"The child is hardly so stout as we could wish," said the doctor. "His mind is too big for his body. He thinks too much. Let him try sea air. Sea air does wonders for children."

So it was arranged that Florence, Paul, and Nurse should go to Brighton, and stay in the house of a lady named Mrs. Pipchin, who kept a very select boarding house for children, and whose management of them was said, in the best circles, to be truly marvelous. Mr. Dombey himself went down to Brighton every week, and had the children to stay with him at his hotel from Saturday to Monday, that he might judge of the progress made by his son and heir towards health.

There is no doubt that, apart from his importance to the house of Dombey and Son, little Paul had crept into his father's heart, cold though it still was towards his daughter, colder than ever now, for there was in it a sort of unacknowledged jealousy of the warm love lavished on her by Paul, which he himself was unable to win.

Mrs. Pipchin was a marvelously ugly old lady, with a hook nose and stern, cold eyes. Two other children lived at present under her charge, a mild blue-eyed little girl who was known as Miss Pankey, and a Master Bitherstone, a solemn and sad-looking little boy whose parents were in India, and who asked Florence in a depressed voice whether she could give him any idea of the way back to Bengal.

"Well, Master Paul, how do you think you will like me?" said Mrs. Pipchin, seeing the child intently regarding her.

"I don't think I shall like you at all," replied Paul, shaking his head. "I want to go away. I do not like your house."

Paul did not like Mrs. Pipchin, but he would sit in his armchair and

look at her, just as he had looked at his father at home. Her ugliness seemed to fascinate him.

As the weeks went by little Paul grew more healthy looking, but he did not seem any stronger, and could not run about out of doors. A little carriage was therefore got for him, in which he could be wheeled down to the beach, where he would pass the greater part of the day. He took a great fancy to a queer crab-faced old man, smelling of seaweed, who

wheeled his carriage, and held long conversations with him. But Florence was the only child-companion whom he ever cared to have with him, though he liked to watch other children playing in the distance. To have Florence sitting by his side, reading or talking to him, while the fresh salt wind blew about him, and the little waves rippled up under the wheels of his carriage, seemed to perfectly content little Paul.

"I love you, Floy," he said one day to her. "If you went to India as that boy's sister did, I should die."

Florence laid her head against his pillow, and whispered how much stronger he was growing.

"Oh yes, I know, I am a great deal better," said Paul, "a very great deal better. Listen, Floy. What is it the sea keeps saying?"

"Nothing, dear, it is only the rolling of the waves you hear."

"Yes, but they are always saying something, and always the same thing. What place is over there, Floy?"

She told him there was another country opposite, but Paul said he did not mean that, he meant somewhere much farther away, oh, much farther away. And often he would break off in the midst of their talk to listen to the sea and gaze out towards that country "farther away."

After having lived at Brighton for a year, Paul was certainly much stronger, though still thin and delicate. And on one of his weekly visits, Mr. Dombey observed to Mrs. Pipchin, with pompous condescension, "My son is getting on, madam, he is really getting on. He is six years of age, and six will be sixteen before we have time to look about us." And then he went on to explain that Paul's weak health having kept him back in his studies, which, considering the great destiny before the heir of Dombey and Son, was much to be regretted, he had made arrangements to place him at the educational establishment of Dr. Blimber, which was close by. Florence was, for the present, to remain under Mrs. Pipchin's care and see her brother every week.

Dr. Blimber's school was a great hothouse for the forcing of boys' brains. No matter how backward a boy was, Dr. Blimber could always bring him on, and make a man of him in no time. And Dr. Blimber promised speedily to make a man of Paul.

"Shall you like to be made a man of, my son?" asked Mr. Dombey.

"I'd rather be a child and stay with Floy," answered Paul.

Then a different life began for little Dombey.

Miss Blimber, the doctor's daughter, a learned lady in spectacles, was his special tutor, and from morning till night his poor little brain was forced and crammed, till his head was heavy and always had a dull ache in it, and his small legs grew weak again. Every day he looked a little thinner and a little paler, and became more old-fashioned than ever in his

looks and ways—"old-fashioned" was a distinguishing title which clung to him. He was gentle and polite to everyone, always looking out for small kindnesses which he might do to any inmate of the house. Everyone liked "little Dombey," but everyone down to the footman said with the same kind of tender smile—he was such an old-fashioned boy. "The oddest and most old-fashioned child in the world," Dr. Blimber would say to his daughter; "but bring him on, Cornelia—bring him on."

And Cornelia did bring him on. And Florence, seeing how pale and weary the little fellow looked when he came to her on Saturdays, and how he could not rest from anxiety about his lessons, would lighten his labors a little, and ease his mind by helping him to prepare his week's work. But one day, when his lessons were over, about a fortnight before the commencement of holidays, little Paul laid his weary and aching head against the knee of a schoolfellow of whom he was very fond, and somehow forgot to lift it up again. The first thing he noticed when he opened his eyes was that the window was open, his face and hair were wet with water, and that Dr. Blimber and the usher were both standing looking at him.

"Ah, that's well," said Dr. Blimber as Paul opened his eyes. "And how is my little friend now?"

"Oh, quite well, thank you, sir," answered Paul, but when he got up there seemed something the matter with the floor, and the walls were dancing about, and Dr. Blimber's head was twice its natural size. Toots, the schoolfellow against whom Paul had been leaning, took him up in his arms, and very kindly helped him to bed. Presently the doctor came and looked at him, and said he was not to do any more lessons for the present.

In a few days Paul was able to get up and creep about the house. He wondered sometimes why everyone looked at and spoke so very kindly to him, and was more than ever careful to do any little kindnesses he could think of for them. Even the rough, ugly dog, Diogenes, who lived in the yard, came in for a share of his attentions.

There was to be a party at Dr. Blimber's on the evening before the

boys went home, and Paul wished to remain for this, because Florence was coming, and he wanted her to see how everyone was fond of him. He was to go away with her after the party. Paul sat in a corner of the sofa all evening, and everyone was very kind to him indeed. It was quite extraordinary, Paul thought, and he was very happy. He liked to see how pretty Florence was, and how everyone admired her and wished to dance

with her. When the time came for them to take leave, the whole houseful gathered on the steps to say good-bye to little Dombey and his sister. Toots even opened the carriage door to say it over again.

After resting for a night at Mrs. Pipchin's house, little Paul went home, and was carried straight upstairs to his bed. "Floy, dear," said he to his sister, when he was comfortably settled, "was that Papa in the hall when I was carried in?"

"Yes, dear," answered Florence.

"He didn't cry, did he, Floy, and go into his own room when he saw me?" Florence could only shake her head, and hide her face against his, as she kissed him.

"I should not like to think Papa cried," murmured little Paul, as he went to sleep. He lay in his bed day after day quite happily and patiently, content to watch and talk to Florence. He would tell her his dreams, and how he always saw the sunlit ripples of a river rolling, rolling fast in front of him. Sometimes he seemed to be rocking in a little boat on the water, and its motion lulled him to rest, and then he could be floating away, away to that shore farther off, which he could not see. One day he told Florence that the water was rippling brighter and faster than ever, and that he could not see anything else.

"My own boy, cannot you see your poor father?" said Mr. Dombey, bending over him.

"Oh yes; but don't be so sorry, dear Papa. I am so happy—good-bye, dear Papa." Presently he opened his eyes again, and said, "Floy, mamma is like you, I can see her. Come close to me, Floy, and tell them," whispered the dying boy, "that the face of the picture of Christ on the staircase at school is not divine enough. The light from it is shining on me now, and the water is shining too, and rippling so fast, so fast." The evening light shone into the room, but little Paul's spirit had gone out on the rippling water, and the Divine Face was shining on him from the farther shore.

The Marchioness

Mr. Dick Swiveller had just been engaged as clerk to Mr. Sampson Brass, who was a lawyer, and he found to his amazement that his fellow clerk was no other than Mr. Brass's sister, Miss Sally Brass. Miss Sally was a grim and gaunt personage, and Mr. Swiveller, who was a light-hearted and easygoing individual, found his first morning's work in her society so difficult to get through that when she at last went out and left him alone he sprang off his stool and danced a hornpipe. Presently he heard a knock at the front door, and then there came a rapping of knuckles at the office door.

"Come in," said Dick.

"Oh, please," said a little voice, very low down in the doorway, "will you come and show the lodgings?"

Dick leaned over the table and saw a small girl in a dirty, coarse apron and bib, which left nothing of her visible but her face and feet. She might as well have been dressed in a violin case.

"Why, who are you?" said Dick.

To which the only reply was, "Oh, please, will you come and show the lodgings?"

"I haven't got anything to do with the lodgings," said Dick. "Tell 'em to call again."

"Oh, but please will you come and show the lodgings," returned the child. "Miss Sally said I wasn't to, because people wouldn't believe the attendance was good if they saw how small I was at first."

"This is a queer sort of thing," muttered Dick, rising. "What do you mean to say you are—the cook?"

"Yes. I do plain cooking," replied the child. "I'm housemaid too. I do all the work of the house."

It became evident from mysterious thumping sounds in the passage that the applicant for the lodgings would not wait, so Dick Swiveller showed them, and he saw no more of the small servant that day. But he did not forget her. It troubled him very much that she seemed always to remain under ground and never came to the surface unless the lodger rang

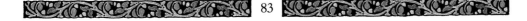

his bell. She never went out, or came into the office, or had a clean face, or took off the coarse apron, or looked out of any of the windows, or stood at the street door for a breath of air, or had any rest or refreshment whatever. Nobody ever came to see her, nobody spoke of her, nobody cared about her.

"Now, I'd give something," said Dick to himself, one day, "I'd give something—if I had it—to know how they treat that child and where they keep her."

The office door was open, and at that moment Dick caught a glimpse of Miss Brass's angular figure flitting down the kitchen stairs. By Jove, thought he, she's going to feed the small servant. Now or never!

First peeping over the handrail and allowing Miss Brass to disappear in the darkness below, he groped his way down, and arrived at the door of a back kitchen immediately after Miss Brass had entered the same, bearing in her hand a cold leg of mutton. It was a very dark, miserable place, very low and very damp. The water was trickling out of a leaking butt, and a most wretched cat was lapping up the drops with the sickly eagerness of starvation. Everything was locked up. The coal cellar, the candle box, the salt box, the meat safe were all padlocked. There was nothing that a beetle could have lunched upon.

The small servant stood with humility in the presence of Miss Sally and hung her head.

"Are you there?" asked Miss Sally.

"Yes, ma'am," was the answer in a weak voice.

"Go farther away from the leg of mutton, or you'll be picking it, I know," said Miss Sally. The child withdrew into a corner while Miss Brass took a key from her pocket and opening the safe brought from it a dreary waste of cold potatoes, looking about as eatable as Stonehenge.

"Do you see this?" said Miss Brass, slicing off about two square inches of cold mutton, holding it out on the point of the fork.

The small servant looked hard enough at it with her hungry eyes to see every shred of it, small as it was, and answered, "Yes."

"Then don't you ever go and say," retorted Miss Sally, "that you hadn't meat here. There, eat it up."

This was soon done. "Now, do you want any more?" said Miss Sally.

The hungry creature answered with a faint "No." They were evidently going through an established form.

Miss Sally put the meat away and locked the safe, and drawing near to the small servant, watched her while she finished the potatoes, rapping her now on her hand, now on her head, and now on her back, as if she found it quite impossible to stand so close to her without administering a few knocks. Then comforting herself with a pinch of snuff, Miss Brass ascended the stairs, just as Dick had safely reached the office.

What he had seen troubled Dick Swiveller very much, and he thought often of the poor small servant. He was left alone a great deal in the office in the evening with nothing to do, and he used to play cribbage by himself.

After a time he began to think that on those evenings he heard a kind of snorting in the direction of the door, which it occurred to him must come from the small servant, who always had a cold from damp living. Looking intently one night he plainly distinguished an eye gleaming and glistening at the keyhole. He stole softly to the door and pounced upon her before she was aware of his approach.

"Oh, I didn't mean any harm, indeed," cried the small servant, struggling like a much larger one. "It's so very dull downstairs. Please don't tell upon me, please don't."

"Tell upon you!" said Dick. "Do you mean to say you were looking through the keyhole for company?"

"Yes, upon my word I was," replied the small servant.

Dick considered a little.

"Well, come in," he said at last. "There, sit down, and I'll teach you how to play cribbage."

"Oh! I durstn't do it," rejoined the small servant. "Miss Sally 'ud kill me if she know'd I come up here."

"Have you got a fire downstairs?" said Dick.

"A very little one," replied the small servant.

"Miss Sally couldn't kill me if she know'd I went down there, so I'll come," said Dick. "Why, how thin you are. Could you eat any bread and meat? Yes? Ah! I thought so. Did you ever taste beer?"

"I had a sip of it once," said the small servant.

"There's a state of things!" cried Mr. Swiveller. "She never tasted it—it can't be tasted in a sip! Why, how old are you?"

"I don't know."

Mr. Swiveller opened his eyes very wide, and vanished straightway.

Presently he returned with a plate of bread and beef and a great pot, and followed his little companion into the kitchen.

"There!" said Dick, putting the plate before her. "First of all, clear that off, and then you'll see what next."

The small servant needed no second bidding, and the plate was soon empty.

"Next," said Dick, handing the pot, "take a pull at that. Well, is it good?"

"Oh, isn't it!" said the small servant.

Mr. Swiveller then took a long draught himself and applied himself to teaching her the game, which she soon learned tolerably well.

"Now," said Mr. Swiveller, putting two sixpences into a saucer and trimming the wretched candle, "those are the stakes. If you win, you get 'em all. If I win, I get 'em. To make it seem more real and pleasant, I shall call you the Marchioness. Do you hear?" The small servant nodded. "Then, Marchioness," said Mr. Swiveller, "fire away!"

The Marchioness, holding her cards very tightly in both hands, considered which to play, and Mr. Swiveller put on the gay and fashionable air which such society required. They played until the striking of ten o'clock reminded Mr. Swiveller that he must go before Mr. Sampson and Miss Sally Brass returned.

"With which object in view, Marchioness," said Mr. Swiveller, gravely, "I shall ask your ladyship's permission to retire from the presence. Marchioness, your health! You will excuse my wearing my hat, but the palace is damp, and the marble floor is—if I may be allowed the expression—sloppy."

As a precaution against this latter inconvenience, Mr. Swiveller had

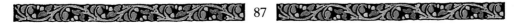

been sitting for some time with his feet on the hob, and now he rose.

"Marchioness," he said, "I am your friend, and I hope we shall play many more games together in this same saloon. But, Marchioness," added Dick, "it occurs to me to ask whether you are in the constant habit of airing your eye at keyholes?"

"I only wanted," replied the trembling Marchioness, "to know where the key of the safe was hid; that was all. And I wouldn't have taken much if I had found it. Only enough to squench my hunger."

"You didn't find it, then?" said Dick. "But of course you didn't, or you'd be plumper. Good night, Marchioness."

Now, after this, strange and sad things happened in Mr. Sampson Brass's office, and Mr. Dick Swiveller left off being his clerk. He was very poor indeed, and he lived in one wretched room, and one night he went home to this room and went to bed and was taken very, very ill.

Tossing to and fro upon his hot, uneasy bed, tormented by a thirst which nothing could appease, dreaming endless, weary dreams, the unfortunate Dick lay wasting inch by inch, until at last he sank into a deep sleep and dreamed no more.

He awoke. With a sensation of most blissful rest, he began to remember something of his sufferings, and to think what a long night it had been, until his attention was attracted by a cough. This made him doubt whether he had locked his door last night. Holding the bed curtains open with one hand, he looked out.

The same room certainly, but with what unbounded astonishment did he see all these bottles and basins and other such furniture of a sick chamber—all very neat and clean, but all quite different from anything he had left there when he went to bed. The atmosphere filled with a cool smell; the floor newly sprinkled; the—the what? The Marchioness? Yes, playing cribbage with herself at the table.

Mr. Swiveller contemplated these things for a short time and then laid his head upon the pillow again.

I'm dreaming, he thought. That's clear.

Not feeling quite satisfied with the explanation, Mr. Swiveller presently raised the bed curtains again. The Marchioness dealt, turned up a knave, and omitted to take the usual advantage. Upon which Mr. Swiveller called out as loud as he could, "Two for his heels!"

The Marchioness jumped up quickly and clapped her hands, and then began to laugh and then to cry, declaring that she was "so glad, she didn't know what to do."

"Marchioness," said Mr. Swiveller, thoughtfully, "be pleased to draw nearer. First of all will you have the goodness to inform me where I shall find my voice; and secondly, what has become of my flesh?" The Marchioness only shook her head mournfully and cried again.

"I begin to infer, Marchioness," said Dick, "that I have been ill."

"You just have!" replied the small servant, wiping her eyes. "Dead, all but! Three weeks tomorrow! Three long, slow weeks."

"Marchioness," said Mr. Swiveller presently, "how's Sally?"

The small servant screwed her face with an expression of the very uttermost entanglement of slyness, and shook her head.

"Bless you," she said, "I've run away."

"And where do you live, Marchioness?"

"Live!" cried the small servant. "Here!"

"Oh!" said Mr. Swiveller.

And with that he lay down flat as suddenly as if he had been shot.

"Tell me," he said, "how was it you thought of coming here?"

"Well, you see," returned the Marchioness, "when you were gone I hadn't any friend at all. But one morning, when I was—"

"Was near a keyhole?" suggested Mr. Swiveller.

"Well, then," said the small servant, nodding, "when I was near the office keyhole, I heard somebody saying that she lived here and that you was took very bad, and wouldn't nobody come and take care of you. Mr. Brass, he says, 'It's no business of mine,' he says. And Miss Sally, she says, 'It's no business of mine.' So I ran away that night, and come here and told 'em you was my brother, and I've been here ever since." "This

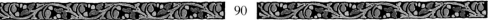

poor little Marchioness has been wearing herself to death!" cried Dick.

"No, I haven't," she returned, "not a bit of it. Don't you mind about me. I'm so glad you're better, Mr. Liverer."

"Liverer, indeed," said Dick, thoughtfully. "It's well I *am* a Liverer. I strongly suspect I should have died, Marchioness, but for you."

From this opinion Mr. Swiveller never departed. Before he had recovered from his illness he inherited some money, and he bought the poor Marchioness a handsome stock of clothes and put her to school forthwith. And when she was nineteen years old they were married, and they played many hundred thousand games of cribbage together. As she had never known her own name, he gave her the name of Sophronia Sphynx. But he called her the Marchioness from first to last.

The Fat Boy

It was at the grand military review that the fat boy first burst in all his glory upon the happy eyes of Mr. Samuel Pickwick, founder and president of the Pickwick Club. Mr. Pickwick was present in the crowd with his three bosom friends—Mr. Tupman, the dandy, Mr. Winkle, the sportsman, and Mr. Snodgrass, the poet—and had grown very tired and hot with long standing, dazzled with watching the marching, wheeling, and counter-marching of regiment after regiment, and nearly deafened by the roar of cheers, the clash of muskets as the troops presented arms, and the noise of brass and pigskin as all the many military bands struck up together. Mr. Pickwick looked round, missing Mr. Tupman, and the next minute missed his hat, which the wind had just blown off his head. It rolled near one of many carriages drawn up in a good position for seeing the troops, and as Mr. Pickwick stooped to pick it up he was hailed from the carriage in Mr. Tupman's hearty voice.

He looked up.

There was a stout gentleman in the carriage with his hand out ready to shake Mr. Pickwick's. There were three ladies, one middle-aged and rather sharp-faced, two young and pretty; there was a young gentleman, there was Mr. Tupman, and on the box, sound asleep, sat the very fattest boy Mr. Pickwick had ever set eyes on. Called to sharply by his master, "Joe—bother that boy, he's gone to sleep again!" he rolled slowly off the box, let down the carriage steps, and held the carriage door invitingly open for the gentlemen. Mr. Winkle mounted to the box, and the fat boy waddled to the same perch and fell fast asleep instantly.

"Joe, Joe!" called Mr. Wardle when the sham fight was over and the sham enemies had gone off to dinner, "time for *us* to feed now, eh, Mr. Pickwick? Bother that boy, he's gone to sleep again. Be good enough to pinch him, sir—in the leg, if you please—nothing else wakes him. Thank you. Undo the hamper, Joe." The fat boy, roused by a smart pinch from Mr. Winkle, rolled off the box once again, and began to unpack the hamper. He looked fondly upon the various eatables as he uncovered them and handed them up to his master. He beamed upon cold beef, sighed over salad, pored upon pigeon pie, and hung so fondly over a plump, cold, roast fowl that he seemed wholly unable to part with it, and his master had almost to tear it away from him. When he had lost it, for good and all, he tried to find comfort in a veal patty, with which he mounted the box once more, where he very soon again fell asleep.

"Does he always sleep in this way?" asked Mr. Pickwick, glancing where he sat nodding on the box.

"Sleep!" said the old gentleman, "he's always asleep. Goes on errands fast asleep, and snores as he waits at table."

"How very odd!" said Mr. Pickwick.

"Odd, indeed!" said Mr. Wardle. "I'm proud of that boy. I wouldn't part with him on any account. He's a natural curiosity. Here, Joe, Joe, take these things away, and help Tom put in the horses."

The fat boy rose, opened his eyes, swallowed the piece of pie which he had been eating when he fell asleep, and slowly obeyed his master's orders, gloating languidly over the remains of the feast as he removed the plates and deposited them in the hamper. The last Mr. Pickwick's party saw of him on that occasion was a fat form nodding on the box as the carriage rattled away.

When they next set eyes upon him it was in the setting of his own home—or, rather, his master's—the Manor Farm, Dingley Dell. This was a house with a great kitchen and a lordly larder. Here he did very little work and ate and drank prodigiously.

Mr. Wardle and his old mother and his two pretty daughters, Isabella and Emily, were very good-natured and indulgent, and of Joe was never asked nor expected anything but the lightest duties.

One of these was to daily lead old Mrs. Wardle (who was very deaf) to a certain arbor in the garden, where she would sit and sun herself in the morning pleasantness.

First of all he had to fetch from a peg behind the old lady's bedroom door a close, black satin bonnet, a warm cotton shawl, and a thick stick. And then the old lady, after having put on the bonnet and shawl at her leisure, would lean one hand on her stick and the other on the fat boy's shoulder, and walk leisurely to the arbor, where the fat boy would leave her to enjoy the fresh air for half an hour. Now, the old lady was very

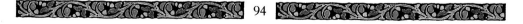

precise and particular, and for three summers there had been no change in this particular form of taking the air, so she was very much scared one morning, during the Pickwick party's visit, to see the fat boy, instead of leaving her in the arbor as usual, look carefully round him and then address her very solemnly, "Missus."

The old lady began to shake. "Well, Joe?" she said, wondering if he meant to rob her of her loose coin, knowing that she was too old and feeble to scream for help. "I'm sure I have been a good mistress to you, Joe. You have never had too much to do, and you have always had enough to eat."

This last appeal went straight to the fat boy's heart.

"I knows I has," he replied.

"Then what can you want to do now?" asked the old lady. The fat boy came closer.

"I wants to make your flesh creep," he said.

"But why?" asked the old lady, trembling again. The fat boy explained. He had seen Miss Rachael—Mrs. Wardle's daughter—in this very arbor with one of Mr. Pickwick's party—Mr. Tracy Tupman, to be exact—kissing her hand.

"And she let him?" cried the old lady. "Miss Rachael—my daughter—she let him?"

The fat boy nodded till his cheeks shook like a jelly.

But if the fat boy could nod, Miss Rachael Wardle could shake her head, and she not only did this, but declared stoutly that what Joe described had never happened, and that he must have dreamed it all.

This for some time put Joe very much out of favor, and any other page boy with any other master would certainly have lost his place. With Mr. Wardle, however, nobody could be long in disgrace, and soon the fat boy was forgiven.

When Christmas time came then, perhaps, the fat boy was at his happiest, for then the biggest fires were kept up, and the richest dishes served in dining room and kitchen alike, and then even the sometimes

cross cook grew good-tempered for the sake of the pleasant season.

And when one Christmas brought a wedding with it—the wedding of pretty Miss Isabella Wardle to a Mr. Trundle—then the fat boy was glorious to see in a new suit, with an enormous white satin favor.

At the wedding breakfast he stole away every now and then to a corner, where, like little Jack Horner of happy memory, he devoured Christmas pies, though, unlike Jack Horner, he wasted none of his valuable time in picking the plums out of them.

On Christmas Eve the family and the servants played games together in the kitchen. A huge bunch of mistletoe was hung up from the kitchen ceiling by Mr. Wardle's own hands, and all the women in the house got kissed underneath it, beginning with the old lady. Then the games began. Blind Man's Buff was the first, and Mr. Pickwick himself was the first to be Blindman. And after that the fat boy came into the kitchen, broad awake for once, carrying a great dish full of flaming brandy and sputtering raisins, and when fingers enough had been burned over snapdragon, they sat down by a great log fire to a good supper and a mighty bowl of wassail, a rich spiced drink of ale and cordials in which roasted apples were hissing and bubbling with a pleasant look and a jolly sound that made everyone who heard and saw them feel as gay as grigs.

Christmas Day itself brought more guests to Manor Farm—gay and noisy young men, who made the fat boy's life a burden to him by disturbing him out of a morning nap with shells of the oysters they had eaten for lunch aimed skilfully at his nodding head as he sat in the chimney corner. After church, however, there was an hour on the ice, when the whole Manor Farm party went off skating, and the fat boy and Sam, Mr. Pickwick's servant, had a very fine time together on a slide that they had made.

By the time Christmastide was over and done with the passing of Twelfth Night, the fat boy was a still fatter boy, and it was a daily puzzle to guess how he managed to fasten together the many little buttons of his page's jacket. March winds, April showers, and May flowers blustered

and fell and blossomed around his Humpty-Dumpty-like figure, and only brought it to a riper roundness; and as for his powers of going to sleep without notice, the advancing year only brought them into greater perfection.

♦ ♦ ♦

Mr. Pickwick and his party had not seen anything of the jolly owner of Manor Farm and the fat boy for some months. Indeed, flighty spring had grown into beautiful summer and summer had ripened into rich autumn when they met again.

Mr. Pickwick was in London at the time—was, indeed, calling at his lawyer's house—when his path and the fat boy's crossed once more.

There came, while the two gentlemen were talking together, a loud and violent knocking at the door, not an ordinary double knock, but a constant supply of the loudest possible single raps, keeping steadily on as if the person outside had learned how to knock but not how to leave off knocking.

The door was opened, and showed them outside a very fat boy standing upright on the mat with his eyes closed in sleep.

The door being opened, Mr. Wardle pushed his way in and shook hands with Mr. Pickwick and the lawyer—who was *his* lawyer too—while the fat boy went to sleep again, as he stood.

Here, standing upright and sleeping soundly and sweetly in the mild October sunshine, we must take our leave of him.

It will be pleasant to think of him as never growing any older.

Never any thinner, always a stout Cupid in buttons with shoulder-straps instead of wings.

Always able to eat heartily and sleep deeply, heart-free and carefree as a young oyster or a young Dutch cheese. Good-bye, Joe.

"Bother that boy, he's asleep again."

Little Dorrit
of the Marshalsea

any years ago, when people could be put in prison for debt, a poor gentleman, who was unfortunate enough to lose all his money, was brought to the Marshalsea prison. As there seemed no prospect of being able to pay his debts, his wife and their two little children came to live there with him. The elder child was a boy of three, the younger a little girl of two years old, and not long afterwards another little girl was born. The three children played in the courtyard, and were happy on the whole, for they were too young to remember a happier state of things.

But the youngest child, who had never been outside the prison walls, was a thoughtful little creature, and wondered what the outside world could be like. Her great friend, the turnkey, who was also her godfather, became very fond of her, and as soon as she could walk and talk, he bought a little armchair and stood it by his fire at the lodge, and coaxed her with cheap toys to come and sit with him. In return the child loved him dearly, and would often bring her doll to dress and undress as she sat in the little armchair. She was still a very tiny creature when she began to understand that everyone did not live locked up inside high walls with spikes at the top, and though she and the rest of the family might pass through the door that the great key opened, her father could not. She would look at him with a wondering pity in her tender little heart.

One day, she was sitting in the lodge gazing wistfully up at the sky through the barred window. The turnkey, after watching her some time, said, "Thinking of the fields, ain't you?"

"Where are they?" she asked.

"Why, they're—over there, my dear," said the turnkey, waving his key vaguely, "just about there."

"Does anybody open them and shut them? Are they locked?"

"Well," said the turnkey, discomfited, "not in general."

"Are they pretty, Bob?" She called him Bob, because he wished it.

"Lovely. Full of flowers. There's buttercups and there's daisies, and there's"—here he hesitated, not knowing the names of many flowers—"there's dandelions, and all manner of games."

"Is it very pleasant to be there, Bob?"

"Prime," said the turnkey.

"Was Father ever there?"

"Hem!" coughed the turnkey. "Oh yes, he was there, sometimes."

"Is he sorry not to be there now?"

"N-not particular," said the turnkey.

"Nor any of the people?" she asked, glancing at the listless crowd within. "Oh are you quite sure and certain, Bob?"

At this point, Bob gave in and changed the subject. But after this chat, the turnkey and little Amy would go out on his free Sunday afternoons to some meadows or green lanes, and she would pick grass and flowers to bring home, while he smoked his pipe. And then they would go to some tea gardens for shrimps and other delicacies, and would come back hand in hand, unless she was very tired and had fallen asleep on his shoulder.

When Amy was only eight years old, her mother died, and the poor father was more helpless and broken down than ever. Since Fanny was a careless child, and Edward idle, the little one, who had the bravest and truest heart, was inspired by her love and unselfishness to be the little mother of the forlorn family. She struggled to get some little education for herself and her brother and sister. She went as often as she could to an evening school outside, and managed to get her brother and sister sent to a day school at intervals, during three or four years.

At thirteen, Amy could read and keep accounts. Once, among the
debtors, a dancing master came in, and as Fanny had a great desire to learn
to dance, little Amy went timidly to the new prisoner, with a bag in her
hand, and said, "If you please, I was born here, sir."

"Oh! You are the young lady, are you?" said he.

"Yes, sir."

"And what can I do for you?"

"Nothing for me, sir, thank you," she replied, anxiously undrawing the strings of the little bag, "but if, while you stay here, you could be so kind as to teach my sister cheap."

"My child, I'll teach her for nothing," said the dancing master, shutting the bag.

Fanny was a very apt pupil, and the good-natured dancing master was so pleased with her progress that he went on giving her lessons after his release, which was not for ten weeks. Amy was so emboldened with the success of her attempt, that when a milliner came in, she went to her on her own behalf, for she had a great desire to learn to do needlework, and begged the milliner to teach her.

"I am afraid you are so weak, you see," the milliner objected.

"I don't think I am weak, ma'am."

"And you are so very, very little, you see," the milliner still objected.

"Yes, I am afraid I am very little indeed," returned the child, and began to sob. The milliner was touched, and taught with good will. She found Amy the most patient and earnest of pupils, and made her a clever workwoman.

But although the father was not too proud to accept "testimonials," in the form of money and presents, from the other debtors who pitied the poor gentleman who seemed doomed to pass his life in that dismal abode, he could not bear the idea that his children should work for their living, so they had to keep it all secret. Fanny became a dancer, and lived with a poor old uncle, who played the clarinet at the small theater where Fanny was engaged. Amy, or Little Dorrit as she was generally called, her father's name being Dorrit, earned small sums by going out to do needlework. She was most anxious to get her brother away from the prison and the bad companions he met there, and helped by her old friend Bob, she got him into a great many situations. But alas! He was an idle, careless fellow, and always came back to be a burden and care to his poor little sister. At last she managed to save up enough to send him out to Canada.

"God bless you, dear Tip" (he had been christened Edward, but it had gradually been shortened to Tip), "don't be too proud to come and see us when you have made your fortune," she said.

But Tip only went as far as Liverpool and after a month on the road he walked back, and appeared once more before his poor little second mother in rags, and with no shoes.

In the end, after another trial, Tip returned, telling Amy that this time he had come back in a new way, as "one of the regulars."

"Oh! Don't say you are a prisoner, Tip. Don't, don't!"

But he was—and it nearly broke Amy's heart. She implored him not to let her father know, because it would kill him, and as Fanny and their uncle joined in her entreaties, he agreed. So with all these cares and worries, struggling bravely on, Little Dorrit passed the first twenty-two years of her life. Then the son of a lady, Mrs. Clennam, to whose house Amy went to do needlework, was interested in the pale, patient little creature, and learning her history resolved to do his best to try to get her father released, and to help them all.

One day when he was walking home with Little Dorrit to try and find out the names of some of the people her father owed money to, a voice was heard calling, "Little Mother, Little Mother," and a strange figure came bouncing up to them and fell down, scattering her basketful of potatoes on the ground. "Oh Maggie," said Little Dorrit, "what a clumsy child you are!"

She was about eight-and-twenty, with large bones, large features, large hands and feet, large eyes and no hair. Little Dorrit explained to Mr. Clennam that Maggie was the granddaughter of her old nurse, who had been dead a long time, and that her grandmother had been very unkind to her and beat her.

"When Maggie was ten years old, she had a fever, and she has never grown older since."

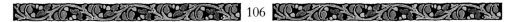

"Ten years old," said Maggie. "But what a nice hospital! So comfortable, wasn't it? Such a Ev'nly place! Such beds there is there! Such lemonades! Such oranges! Such delicious broth and wine! Such Chicken! Oh, *ain't* it a delightful place to stop at!"

"Then when she came out, her grandmother did not know what to do with her, and was very unkind. But after some time, Maggie tried to improve, and was very attentive and industrious, and now she can earn her own living entirely, sir!"

Little Dorrit did not say who had taken pains to teach and encourage the poor girl, but Mr. Clennam guessed from the name Little Mother, and the fondness of the poor creature for Amy.

One cold, wet evening, Little Dorrit and Maggie went to Mr. Clennam's house to thank him for having freed Edward from the prison, and on coming out found it was too late to get home, because the gate was locked. They tried to get in at Maggie's lodgings, but though they knocked twice, the people were asleep. Little Dorrit did not wish to disturb them, so they wandered about all night, sometimes sitting at the gate of the prison, Maggie shivering and whimpering.

"It will soon be over, dear," said patient Amy.

"Oh, it's all very well for you, Mother," said Maggie, "but I'm a poor thing, only ten years old."

Thanks to Mr. Clennam, a great change took place in the fortunes of the family, and not long after this wretched night, he came to tell Mr. Dorrit that he was the owner of a large property, and so they became very rich.

But Little Dorrit never forgot, as, sad to say, the rest of the family did, the friends who had been kind to them in their poverty. And when, in his turn, through no fault of his own, Mr. Clennam became a prisoner in the Marshalsea, Little Dorrit came to comfort and console him, and after a while she became his wife, and they lived happy ever after.

Little Nell
and Her Grandfather

The house was one of those receptacles for old and curious things, which seem to crouch in odd corners of London town. In the old, dark, murky rooms, there lived together alone an old man and a child—his grandchild, little Nell. Solitary and monotonous as was her life, the innocent and cheerful spirit of the child found happiness in all things, and through the dim rooms of the old curiosity shop little Nell went singing, moving with a light step.

But gradually over the old man, to whom she was so tenderly attached, there stole a sad change. He became thoughtful, dejected, and wretched. He had no sleep nor rest but that which he took by day in his easy chair. For every night, and all night long, he was away from home. To the child it seemed that her grandfather's love for her increased, even with the hidden grief by which she saw him struck down. And to see him sorrowful, and not to know the cause of his sorrow, to see him growing pale and weak under his agony of mind, so weighed upon her gentle spirit, that at times she felt as though her heart must break.

At last the time came when the old man's feeble frame could bear up no longer against his hidden care. A raging fever seized him, and as he lay delirious or insensible through many weeks, Nell learned that the house which sheltered them was theirs no longer. In the future they would be very poor. They would scarcely have bread to eat.

At length the old man began to mend, but his mind was weakened. He would sit for hours together, with Nell's small hand in his,

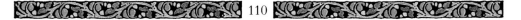

playing with the fingers, and sometimes stopping to smooth her hair or
kiss her brow. And when he saw that tears were glistening in her eyes he
would look amazed. As the time drew near when they must leave the
house, he made no reference to the necessity of finding other shelter. He
had an indistinct idea that the child was desolate, and in need of help,

though he seemed unable to contemplate their real position more distinctly. But a change came upon him one evening, as he and Nell sat quietly together.

"Let us speak softly, Nell," he said. "Hush! for if they knew our purpose they would say that I was mad, and take thee from me. We will not stay here another day. We will travel afoot through the fields and woods, and trust ourselves to God in the places where He dwells. To-morrow morning, dear, we'll turn our faces from this scene of sorrow, and be as free and happy as the birds."

The child's heart beat high with hope and confidence. She had no thought of hunger, or cold, or thirst, or suffering. To her it seemed that they might beg their way from door to door in happiness, so that they were together.

When the day began to glimmer they stole out of the house, and passing into the street stood still.

"Which way?" asked the child.

The old man looked irresolutely and helplessly at her, and shook his head. It was plain that she was thenceforth his guide and leader. The child felt it, but had no doubts nor misgivings, and, putting her hand in his, led him away. Forth from the city, while it yet slumbered, went the two poor adventurers, wandering they knew not where.

They passed through the long, deserted streets, in the glad light of early morning, until these streets dwindled away, and the open country was about them. They walked all day, and slept that night at a small cottage where beds were let to travelers. The sun was setting on the second day of their journey, and they were worn out with walking, when, following a path which led through a churchyard to the town where they were to spend the night, they fell in with two traveling showmen, exhibitors of a Punch and Judy show, bound for the races at a neighboring town. And with these men they traveled forward on the following day.

They made two long days' journey with their new companions,

passing through villages and towns, and meeting upon one occasion with two young people walking upon stilts, who were also going to the races. The men were rough and strange, in their ways, but they were kindly too; and in the tumult and confusion of such scenes as little Nell had never known before, and in the bewildering noise and movement of the race-course, where she tried to sell some little nosegays, Nell would have clung to them for protection, had she not learned that these men suspected that she and the old man had left their home secretly, and that they meant to take steps to have them sent back and taken care of. Separation from her grandfather was Nell's greatest fear. If they should be found (so the child thought), people would shut him from the light of sun and sky, saying that he was mad, and never let her see him again. She seized her opportunity to evade the watchfulness of the two men, and hand in hand she and the old man fled away together.

That night they reached a little village in a woody hollow. The village schoolmaster, a good and gentle man, pitying their weariness, and attracted by the child's sweetness and modesty, gave them a lodging for the night; nor would he let them leave him until two days more had passed.

They journeyed on, when the time came that they must wander forth again, by pleasant country lanes. As they passed, watching the birds that perched and twittered in the branches overhead, or listening to the songs that broke the happy silence, their hearts were tranquil and serene. But by and by they came to a long winding road which lengthened out far into the distance, and though they still kept on, it was at a much slower pace, for they were now very weary.

The afternoon had worn away into a beautiful evening, when they came to a caravan drawn up by the road. It was a smart little house upon wheels, and at the door sat a stout and comfortable lady, taking tea. The tea things were set out upon a drum, covered with a white napkin. And there, as if at the most convenient table in the world, sat this roving lady, taking her tea and enjoying the view. Of this stout lady Nell ventured to ask how far it was to the neighboring town. And the lady, being kindhearted, and noticing that the tired child could hardly repress a tear at hearing that eight weary miles lay still before them, not only gave them tea, but offered to take them on in the caravan.

Now this lady of the caravan was the owner of a waxwork show, and her name was Mrs. Jarley. And Mrs. Jarley was won, as the poor

schoolmaster had been, by Nell's gentle looks and manner. She offered Nell employment in pointing out the figures in the waxwork show to the visitors who came to see it, promising in return both board and lodging for the child and her grandfather, and some small sum of money. This offer Nell was thankful to accept, and for some time her life and that of the poor, vacant, fond old man passed quietly and almost happily.

But heavier sorrow was yet to come. One night, a holiday night for them, Nell and her grandfather went out to walk. There was a terrible thunderstorm and they were forced to take refuge in a small public house. Here some sinister and ill-favored men were playing cards. The old man watched them with increasing interest and excitement, until his whole appearance underwent a complete change. His face was flushed and eager, his teeth set. With a hand that trembled violently, he seized Nell's little purse, and in spite of her entreaties joined in the game, gambling with such a savage thirst for gain that the distressed and frightened child could almost better have borne to see him dead. The night was far advanced before the play came to an end, and they were forced to remain where they were until the morning. And in the night the child was wakened from her troubled sleep to find a figure in the room—a figure busying its hands about her garments, while its face was turned to her, listening and looking lest she should awake. It was her grandfather himself, his white face pinched and sharpened by the greediness which made his eyes unnaturally bright, counting the money of which his hands were robbing her.

Evening after evening, after that night, the old man would steal away, not to return until the night was far spent, wildly demanding money. And at last there came an hour when the child overheard him, tempted beyond his feeble powers of resistance, undertake to find more money, to feed the desperate passion which had laid its hold upon his weakness, by robbing Mrs. Jarley.

That night the child took her grandfather by the hand and led him away. Through the straight streets and narrow outskirts of the town their trembling feet passed quickly. The child was sustained by the idea that they were flying from disgrace and crime, and that her grandfather's preservation must depend solely upon her firmness unaided by one word of advice or any helping hand. The old man followed her as though she had been an angel messenger sent to lead him where she would.

The hardest part of all their wanderings was now before them. They slept in the open air that night, and on the following morning some men offered to take them a long distance on their barge. These men, though they were not unkind, were very rugged, noisy fellows, and they drank and quarreled fearfully among themselves, to Nell's inexpressible terror. It rained, too, heavily, and she was wet and cold. At last they reached the great city whither the barge was bound, and here they wandered up and down, being now penniless, and watched the faces of those who passed, to find among them a ray of encouragement or hope. Ill in body, and sick to death at heart, the child needed her utmost firmness and resolution even to creep along.

They laid down that night, and the next night too, with nothing between them and the sky. A penny loaf was all they had had that day, and when the third morning came, it found the child much weaker, yet she made no complaint. The great manufacturing city hemmed them in on every side, and seemed to shut out hope. Faint and spiritless as they were, its streets were insupportable. The child, throughout the remainder of that hard day, compelled herself to press on, that they might reach the country. Evening was drawing on. They were dragging themselves through the last street, and she felt that the time was close at hand when her enfeebled powers would bear no more. Seeing a traveler on foot before them, and animated with a ray of hope, she shot on before her grandfather, and began in a few faint words to implore the stranger's help. He turned his head, the child clapped her hands together, uttered a wild shriek, and fell senseless at his feet. It was the village schoolmaster who had been so kind to them before.

And now Nell's weary wanderings were nearly over. The good man

took her in his arms and carried her quickly to a little inn nearby. She was tenderly put to bed, and a doctor arrived with all speed. The schoolmaster, as it appeared, was on his way to a new home. And when the child had recovered somewhat from her exhaustion, it was arranged that she and her grandfather should accompany him to the village where he was bound, and that he should try to find them some humble occupation by which they could subsist.

It was a secluded village, lying among the quiet country scenes Nell loved. And here, her grandfather being tranquil and at rest, a great peace fell upon the spirit of the child. Often she would steal into the church, and sitting down among the quiet figures carved upon the tombs, would think of the summer days and the bright springtime that would come, of the rays of sun that would fall in, aslant those sleeping forms, of the songs of birds, and the sweet air that would steal in. What if the spot awakened thoughts of death? It would be no pain to sleep amid such sights and sounds as these. For the time was drawing nearer every day when Nell was to rest indeed. She never murmured or complained, but faded like a light upon a summer's evening and died. Day after day and all day long, the old man, broken-hearted and with no love or care for anything in life, would sit beside her grave with her straw hat and the little basket she used to carry, waiting till she should come to him again. At last they found him lying dead upon the stone. And in the church where they had often prayed and mused and lingered, hand in hand, the child and the old man slept together.